Lost in Spain

1642622   1500

by John Wilson

Fitzhenry & Whiteside

Fitzhenry & Whiteside Limited
195 Allstate Parkway
Markham, Ontario
L3R 4T8

In the United States (queries only):
121 Harvard Avenue, Suite 2
Allston, Massachusetts 02134

www.fitzhenry.ca
godwit@fitzhenry.ca

Fitzhenry & Whiteside acknowledges with thanks the support of the Government of Canada
through its Book Publishing Industry Development Program.

Printed in Canada.

Cover design by Kerry Designs.
Cover illustration by Don Kilby.

10 9 8 7 6 5 4 3 2 1

Canadian Cataloguing in Publication Data
Wilson, John (John Alexander), 1951-
Lost in Spain

ISBN 1-55041-550-6 (bound) ISBN 1-55041-523-9 (pbk.)

I. Title.
PS8595.I5834L67 2000   jC813'.54   C99-931302-9
PZ7.W54Lo 2000

For Dorothy Anne Murnaghan

(1934-1999)

Spanish History Timeline

1924-1930: Primo de Rivera rules as dictator of Spain.

1931-1936: Spain is a Republic, but rising demands for autonomy from the many regions of Spain—particularly the Basque Provinces and Catalonia—and political conflict keep the country unstable.

1936-1939: Spanish Civil War

Fought between the political right (the Nationalists or Rebels)—which consists of the Catholic Church, wealthy landowners, most of the professional classes and the military—and the left-wing Popular Front government (the Republicans)—which consists of the Basque and Catalan Separatists, Socialists, Communists, Anarchists, and the many rural peasants.

July 17, 1936: General Franco leads Spanish army revolt in Morocco.

July 18-20, 1936: Nationalists revolt across Spain.

July 20, 1936: Republic appeals to France for aid.

July 28, 1936: German planes begin ferrying Franco's elite troops from Morocco to Spanish mainland.

July 30, 1936: Italy sends 12 bombers to the rebels.

August 8, 1936: France closes border with Spain.

October 1936: Franco becomes head of the Nationalists. Fascist Italy and Nazi Germany support the rebels.

November 1936: Nationalists besiege Madrid; International Brigades begins fighting for the Republic.

1937: International Brigades and Republicans repulse Nationalists at the Battle of Guadalajara, outside Madrid.

April 1937: Franco organizes Fascist Falange and other right-wing groups under his command. German bombing of Guernica causes many deaths and massive destruction.

May 1937: Marxists revolt in Barcelona, oust Socialist Premier Largo Caballero and destroy POUM. Juan Negrin leads new republican government.

June 1937: Last republican stronghold in the North—Bilbao—falls to the Nationalists. Canadian volunteers organize into the Mackenzie-Papineau Battalion of the International Brigades.

December 1937: Republicans win Battle of Teruel.

February 1938: Fall of Malagata to Nationalists.

March-June 1938: Nationalist forces split republican territory in two.

July 1938: Battle of the Ebro—last republican offensive of the war.

November 1938: International Brigades withdrawn from Spain.

1939: Britain and France recognize Franco regime.

January 1939: Barcelona falls to Franco. Nationalists take control of Catalonia

March 1939: Negrin's Republican government is overthrown during a military coup. The new government seeks to end war, but peace overtures are rejected by Nationalists. Nationalists capture Madrid. Republic surrenders. Civil war ends.

1939-1975: Franco is dictator of Spain.

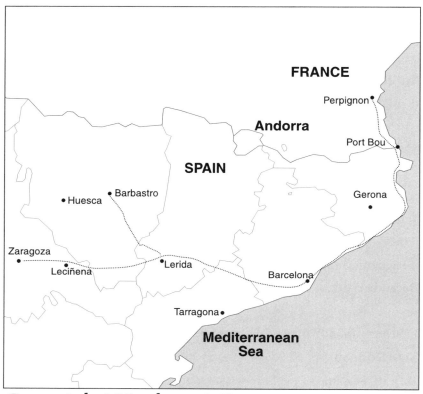

Spanish Workers' Organizations

CNT (Confederación Nacional del Trabajo) –
National Federation of Workers—Anarchists.

FAI (Federación Anarquista Ibérica) –
Spanish Anarchist Federation.

POUM (Partido Obrero de Unificatión Marxista) –
Trotskyist Communists.

PSUC (Partido Socialista Unificado de Cataluna) –
The United Catalan Socialist Party—Stalinist Communists.

UGT (Unión General de Trabajadores) –
Union of Workers—Socialist.

Tuesday, June 5, 1935

⁘————————⁘

"I'd take you if I could. You know that!"

Will Ryan stood on the dusty railway platform of Salmon Arm in the center of British Columbia. It was early afternoon. Around him milled a crowd of men in cloth caps and ragged, patched clothes. Behind him a freight train stood beside the platform, steam hissing from its engine.

Men were clambering on board, trying to find a place on the already overcrowded wagons.

"Ted," Will continued, "you have to understand that I can't take you any farther. It's too dangerous. It's going to get cold in the mountains and there won't be much air in those long tunnels. Then there's the cops. Everyone says it's 'On-To-Ottawa,' but I doubt the police and their bully-boys will let us get that far. There's bound to be trouble somewhere along the line."

Down the platform a whistle sounded. The train jerked noisily and began to move slowly eastward. Men jumped aboard as it gathered speed. Someone shouted, "Come on boys! You don't want to miss the fun."

Will glanced over his shoulder.

"I have to go," he said. "Get onto the road south and stick out your thumb. There's plenty farmers who will pick you up. You'll be home before you know it.

"Take care, Ted," he added reaching forward to ruffle his son's hair.

Then Will was gone. Just one figure among many in a crowded open wagon.

Ted waved at his father. With his spare hand he smoothed down his hair. He hated when his father ruffled it like that. Didn't he realize Ted was 14, almost a man? Hair ruffling was something you did to little kids.

Ted turned and moved onto the road with the remnants of the crowd. It was over, the best week of his life.

Seven days in Vancouver. It was the largest, most vibrant place Ted had ever been and he soaked up as much of the atmosphere as he could—the busy harbor, Chinatown, the fancy cars and well-dressed people downtown. Then there were the political meetings—smoky, noisy, overcrowded halls filled with angry men calling for violent revolution. And always, in the background, the police—watching.

"The biggest enemy is silence," Will would say. "When Adrian Arcand leads his fascists through the streets of Montreal, anyone who doesn't stand up and say 'This is wrong,' is just as much to blame as the thug who breaks a Jewish shopkeeper's window. Not everyone is a fascist, but if no one says anything against them, we might as well all be."

Ted didn't understand it all. How could something Will said at a union meeting in Vancouver make any difference to a Jewish shopkeeper in Montreal? But he was learning that the world Will was trying to change was a complex place.

Ted sighed and moved along the road. It had been a great adventure, but now it was over. "When will the next one be?" he wondered idly.

Saturday, July 18, 1936
Afternoon

Ted leaned against the ancient stones of Perpignan castle and luxuriated in the sun's warmth. This was the life. Shielding his eyes against the brightness, he peered over the gray stone battlements. In the distance, across the flat plain with its neatly ordered fields of cabbages, beets and carrots, past the winding silver streak of the Tet river, he could see the sunlit glitter of the Mediterranean Sea. If he turned and squinted in the opposite direction Ted could just make out the distant hazy line of the Pyrenees Mountains. From the street below, the sounds of fruit and vegetable vendors touting their wares lazily drifted up. Maybe later he would try out his rudimentary French and buy an orange. But not right now. Right now, tired after a morning exploring the city's ancient mysteries, Ted felt like basking on a rock for a while. He closed his eyes.

This was definitely the best holiday Ted had ever had: Toronto, then ten days on the transatlantic steamer to London, a week in Paris, and now Perpignan in the south of France, right up against the Spanish border. In three days he would be on his way to Barcelona and then, if he could work his way around his mother, he would see his first bullfight.

It was all like an unbelievable dream come true—much better than his week in Vancouver. That had been exciting enough, but it had all ended badly. As his dad had predicted, the cops did try to stop the "On-To-Ottawa" trek. In Regina, the men were hauled off the train. Later, at a demonstration, there had been violence. The police had opened fire, killing at least one man. Ted's mother had been worried sick. When his father eventually arrived home, there had been arguments and raised voices.

"That was irresponsible Will," Ted's mother had said, "taking Ted on the train in the first place, dropping him off in Salmon Arm, miles from home, and then deserting us for weeks. On top of it all you could have been killed, then where would we have been?"

"But Catherine, that's exactly why I sent him home—so he would be out of danger."

That night there had been a big fight. Ted had lain, swamped by confusion, listening to the raised voices through the wall. He understood his father's passion for social change, yet he agreed with his mother about Will's irresponsibility. The next day at school, things became even worse.

Ted was tired and anxious. He wasn't looking for trouble, but the first person he ran into was Henry Thomas. Henry's dad owned the shoe store in town and made no bones about disagreeing with Will on almost everything. Henry seemed to take equal pleasure in jumping down Ted's throat at the least provocation. He was always saying what a great guy Hitler was—making Germany efficient and building good roads and cars and so on. Ted would counter with what he knew about the concentration camps and the laws against the Jews, but the two usually ended up coming to blows. Or at least Henry did. Ted tried his hardest not to respond.

"If you hit back," Will had said when they had talked about the problem, "you are descending to his level of violence. You become no better than Henry Thomas. There is a man in India—Gandhi—who is standing up to the entire might of the British Empire with non-violence. He and his followers don't fight back when they are attacked by the police. They stand and let themselves be beaten. And do you know what? Often the police stop. It is very difficult to hit another human being if he is unarmed and unresisting."

Unfortunately, Henry Thomas had never heard of Gandhi. It seemed that the less Ted responded, the more he encouraged Henry. Mostly Henry just pushed and shoved Ted, but lately, Henry was becoming more aggressive and had begun punching Ted. Not very hard, and it didn't really hurt much, but Ted was getting a reputation amongst his friends as a wimp, and that hurt. Ted tried to explain pacifism, but words that sounded strong and noble from his dad, sounded like weak excuses when Ted said them.

The other problem was that even though Ted didn't
respond to Henry, on the occasions when they ended up in
front of a teacher or the principal, Ted was always blamed for
starting the disturbance. He was developing a reputation as a
trouble-maker. It was all horribly unfair.

That morning, Ted had just turned into the schoolyard.
He wasn't really paying attention to what was going on
around him.

"Well, the cops showed your dad and his cronies this
time, eh?"

Ted looked up to see Henry standing before him with a
self-satisfied grin on his face. Ted tried to ignore the chal-
lenge, but Henry blocked his way.

"Ain't gonna be no revolution here," he said triumphantly.
"Commies like your dad are just gonna learn why cops carry
billy-clubs."

"He's not a communist, he's a socialist," said Ted. He
changed direction but Henry moved with him.

"So you say. But they're all the same 'far as I can see.
Trouble-making riff-raff, and the worst is old Will Ryan."

Ted ducked to try and weave past.

"Pity we ain't in Germany. I reckon old Hitler'd know
what to do with the likes of your dad."

Ted gritted his teeth and tried to push past Henry.

"Push me will you," Henry pushed back hard and Ted
staggered a couple of steps. A small crowd was beginning to

gather.

"You're a wimp, Ted Ryan," Henry spat out, "just like your father."

"Hit him Ted," someone in the crowd shouted.

Ted stepped to the side. He didn't even see Henry's fist coming. All he felt was a stinging blow to his chin and suddenly he was lying dazed on his back, and Henry Thomas was circling him with fists clenched.

"Come on, get up and fight," Henry said through clenched teeth.

Ted was close to tears. He knew he could probably beat Henry Thomas. Though small, Ted was wiry, quick and surprisingly strong. Henry was a bullying tub of lard who would cave as soon as someone stood up to him. The problem was, Ted was more afraid of disappointing Will than he was of Henry or the taunts of his friends.

The crowd parted and two teachers came through.

"Ryan and Thomas, fighting again," one of them said. "Come on, principal's office for you."

As usual, Ted got detention and Henry got a warning.

Ted's parents disagreed about the fights. Will was proud of Ted for not backing down or resorting to violence. Catherine was worried that Ted was becoming a "bad kid," who wouldn't be able to get good grades and make something of his life. It worried Ted that life was turning out to be so complicated.

Still, life didn't seem such a problem now that Ted was in Europe basking in the Mediterranean sun while Henry sweated back in his father's store. It was incredible how much had changed in the year since that fight, and it was all because of the inheritance from Uncle Roger.

Roger had been Ted's mother's younger brother, and her only surviving relative. Her father had been killed in the First World War and her mother had died in the great influenza epidemic of 1919. The following year, Catherine had emigrated to Canada, where she had met and married Will. Roger had stayed behind in Britain and done very well for himself. He had struggled at first but eventually prospered at what Ted's mother referred to as "the import/export business."

Ted had only met his uncle a couple of times, but Roger had left a lasting impression. The last time had been in 1934 when Roger had stayed with them for a few days on his way to Asia. Ted remembered a tall man with a young face, prematurely gray hair and a ready smile. What had most impressed Ted, however, had been Roger's clothes. They were new, and the knees and seat of his trousers looked like they had never come in contact with the ground, unlike the broad shiny patches on Will's only suit. Roger had shirts that were always white and pressed, sweaters without any darn patches, and bright ties which seemed to emerge in endless profusion from the depths of two shiny, leather suitcases.

Ted decided that Uncle Roger was rich, which explained

why he and his father didn't seem to get along very well. Will didn't have much time for rich people, especially those who didn't do anything worthwhile with their money— squandering it all, as Roger seemed to be doing, on exotic travel and frivolous luxuries. Ted knew it was wrong for Roger to ignore the plight of the poor and the workers, but he couldn't help admiring their visitor: admiring Roger's clothes, his easygoing style, his laughter and jokes, and the way he could make Ted's mother's eyes sparkle with his tales of far-off places. Ted loved the tales too, especially the ones about castles in Europe, princes and elephants in India, and exotic strangers on South Sea islands. They fed Ted's dreams and convinced him that one day he would travel the world—just for a few years, then he would come back to lead the worker's revolution.

So, when the telegram arrived telling them Uncle Roger had died, the family was shocked. In fact, Catherine had been devastated, and for days had dissolved into tears at the least provocation.

Two weeks after the telegram, a letter had arrived from a lawyer in London giving more details of what had happened. Roger's plane had crashed in the North African desert. During take-off, something had gone wrong. The plane had flipped over, trapping Roger and the pilot. As the ground crew ran to help, the fuel tanks had exploded, enveloping the wreck in flames. No one had been able to get close enough to pull the burning men free. There was no way anyone could have lived through the inferno. The fire had been so intense, all that remained were a few teeth and charred bones. Ted was haunted by the horrific image of Roger trapped and burning with help so close at hand. Ted felt a sense of loss stronger than he would have imagined for someone he never really knew.

The crash had not been the only news in the letter, though. It seemed that Roger had been fairly rich after all and he had left a sizable chunk of his money to Catherine. It was not enough for the Ryans to move to Vancouver and live in style, but it was more than any of them had seen in years of struggle, and it would allow them to do something interesting.

That something had been the cause of considerable discussion. First, it was agreed that the money would be divided into three sections: one to buy immediate necessities like new clothes and shoes; another to be put into savings for a rainy day; and the last section to be used for something special. Will had made a pitch for a donation to the local community hall, but did not push too hard when Catherine said no. She wanted to use the money for a holiday, which Ted had to admit was a better idea. Will hesitated, but had come around when they figured out that, if careful, there would be enough for a trip to Europe the following summer.

So here they were and Ted was loving every minute of it.

Europe's strangeness was so exciting that every waking moment was a thrill and every night was filled with wonderful dreams. Then there was the visit to Spain. Ted had wanted desperately to go to a bullfight ever since he had taken a break from his beloved western novels to devour a tattered copy of Hemingway's *Death in the Afternoon*. Though a hard read, Ted had been enthralled by Hemingway's stories of brave bulls and valiant matadors, the grainy photographs and strange-sounding names like Maera, Joselito and Belmonte. Ted swore to himself that one day he would experience the thing itself.

Will had been okay with the idea and had even filled in a lot of the background on Spain—how its people were emerging from under the darkness of dictatorship and holding up a bright lantern for everyone else in Europe. Catherine had not been so enthusiastic. She didn't like the violence of bullfights and, despite Ted's best efforts to explain the different perspective put forward by Hemingway, deplored the way the horses were killed in the process. Ted had not pushed too hard because, until now, it had just been a dream. But, here they were, minutes from the Spanish border—and the realization of this dream. The tension was almost unbearable.

Resetting his cap, Ted stood up and stretched. He felt refreshed, but it was beginning to get really hot. Time to head back to the guest house where his family congregated every afternoon for a siesta before setting out for an evening of exploration.

Ted ran down the worn steps into the bustle of the market. A few centimes and some halting phrases bought him an orange, which he sucked on as he headed through the narrow streets. The crowds were beginning to thin out in the heat but, oddly, Ted noticed knots of men gathered round the tiny, overcrowded newsstands which decorated every corner. Ted couldn't remember seeing this before—in fact, he didn't think the papers even came out at this time of day. The crowds around the stands were agitated and there was much arm waving and excited talk. Ted couldn't understand the French headlines, but he did notice *"L'ESPAGNE,"* which he knew meant Spain. He hurried away making a mental note to ask his dad what was going on.

Saturday, July 18, 1936
Evening

T ed didn't have to ask his father anything. The moment he entered the high, cool chamber of their room he knew something was seriously wrong. It was obvious from the way the silence fell when he opened the door, and by the way his parents looked at him, that they were discussing something of extreme importance.

"Where have you been?" his mother was first to break the silence. She sounded worried.

"Just wandering around," Ted answered. "I spent some time at the old castle. I told you I was going there this morning," he concluded a bit lamely.

"Well don't go out again without us. We're going home as soon as we can."

Ted was stunned.

"Home!" he exclaimed. "Why? We can't. We've got our tickets for the train to Barcelona on Tuesday. Our holiday's not over yet."

"Calm down, Ted," Will said. "Your mother's right. Things have changed in Spain, you are going to have to go home."

"Why?" Ted repeated, feeling close to tears. "What's changed?"

"Everything," said Will, gesturing for Ted to sit down on the edge of the bed. "There's a revolution going on in Spain. The army in Morocco revolted against the government yesterday. They shot those who wouldn't help them. Today it appears the revolt has spread to the mainland. Seville, Córdoba and Pamplona are already in army hands and there are reports on the radio of street fighting in Madrid and Barcelona. Nobody knows exactly what is happening, but there's no way we can go on with our holiday."

Ted sat down heavily on the bed. So much for his bullfight dream.

"So, what are we going to do?" he asked.

"Well," Will glanced at Catherine "I went down to the railway station and exchanged your tickets for ones to Paris."

"Our tickets," Ted interrupted. "What about yours? Aren't you coming with us? Why are you staying here?"

"He's not staying here," Ted's mother looked tired. "He's going to Barcelona."

"Just for a few days," Will was glancing back and forth between them. "To see what's going on. I'll catch up with you in Paris or London and we can all go home together."

Ted was horrified. In minutes his life had been turned upside down. Instead of a dream holiday, this was turning into a nightmare. His father was abandoning him to go off to some war. He and his mother were being cast adrift to fend for themselves in some strange place where they didn't even speak the language. Feelings of disappointment, anger and frustration surged through Ted. He felt hot tears running down his cheeks.

"How could you," he choked out. Moving unsteadily, he ran across the room, flung open the door and fled down the stairs into the street. Without thinking where he was going, and with the world blurred by his tears, he stumbled over the rough cobblestones, bumping into people, heedless of their angry shouts. He was crying uncontrollably now and ran only to escape.

At last, after many turns and an almost fatal trip across the main thoroughfare of the town, Ted found himself in a small square. It looked very old. In the center was a fountain topped with a statue of a sea serpent twined around a rock. Water gushed out of the monster's mouth. Apartment doorways and a few small cafés were scattered around the edges of the square. At rickety-looking tables, old men sat drinking and smoking. In one corner of the square a group of men were intent upon a game of bowls. No one paid much attention to the Canadian boy who suddenly appeared in their midst and sat down, exhausted and tearful, on the rim of the fountain.

After a while, Ted regained his breath. He was running

out of tears but he still felt totally dejected. It seemed like his world was falling apart, although, when he looked at the situation rationally, Ted knew this was ridiculous. Going home would not be too bad. There would be the missed bullfight, but the holiday up to now had been more than he had ever dreamed possible and they could probably do other things on the way back. No, the real problem was Will. Why did he have to split up the family? It had been great being together for the last few weeks. There had been the occasional meetings with left-wing sympathizers in England and Paris, but Will had been available to talk to Ted about other things—not just socialism. Will knew vast amounts about history, geography and the cultures of Europe, and he could tell an excellent story, making even an old pile of stones come alive into walls that had seen the Roman legions march past.

Will had not just been available to Ted. He had been paying a lot more attention to Catherine as well. Occasionally, Ted had surprised them in a passionate kiss when they thought he wasn't around and, on a few evenings, they had gone out to eat on their own, leaving Ted to fend for himself. There hadn't even been a single fight since they had arrived. It was so very different from life back home, and here was Will destroying it with some crazy idea about going off to a war that was none of his business. Angrily Ted splashed his hand in the fountain, causing some of the old men to glance over at him.

"Hitting water won't do you much good," the voice made Ted jump. He looked up to see Will standing across the fountain from him, a slight smile on his lips. "Mind if I join you?"

Will came round and sat down beside Ted who stubbornly returned his gaze to the surface of the water.

"You know, this fountain's very old," Will continued. "It dates back to when there were pirates around here. They came from the islands or from Africa and they used to raid the towns up and down the coast, capturing ships in the harbor. The story goes that one day the pirates were planning a major raid on Perpignan. Though the townsfolk heard about the raid in advance, there was little they could do, except hide behind the town walls. But they weren't soldiers and the pirates would probably find a way through if they were determined enough. In any case, the countryside around would be devastated, which would probably lead to famine the next winter."

Ted felt himself being drawn into the story despite himself. He still refused to lift his head, but he was listening intently as Will continued.

"It was a fine calm day when the pirates were finally spotted by the lookouts. The news spread panic in the town. People ran everywhere trying to bury their treasures and lock themselves in their houses. Just when it seemed that nothing could stop the pirates, a huge wave appeared on the horizon, moving at a fantastic speed and growing in size as it approached. The pirate ships were caught in the shallow waters of the estuary and thrown up onto the land. Very few of them escaped. It is said that the wave reached as far as the town walls before it retreated. So Perpignan was saved. Even the fishermen and farmers who should have been in their boats or fields were saved because they were hiding inside the town.

"Word got around that the miraculous wave had been the work of a benevolent sea monster, so the grateful citizens built this fountain to honor and thank it for saving them. If you look closely, it seems to be a particularly friendly monster. It almost looks as if it's smiling."

Despite himself, Ted looked up. The monster did indeed seem to be smiling down at him.

"Of course," his father continued, "the wave was probably a tsunami caused by some earthquake at the other end of the Mediterranean, but nobody's ever built a fountain to honor an earthquake before."

"Why do you have to go, Dad?" Ted blurted out. "We're having such a great time and we're like a real family now, doing things together and all. Why are you going to wreck it?"

"I don't want to wreck it, Ted," Will replied slowly. "I'm enjoying this holiday as much as you, and it is wonderful to see your mom relax so much. But this is important. If this thing in Spain turns into a long, drawn-out struggle, which I suspect it will, then the shots fired in Madrid today might be the first shots of a much bigger war. The Spanish generals who started the revolt are fascist. They want to destroy the freely-elected government and drag Spain back into the past—to have it ruled by themselves, the rich landowners and the corrupt Church. They want to kill anyone who opposes them and crush free speech.

"Hitler and Mussolini will help these fascists if they need it. Then the democracies in France and England, and maybe even Stalin in Russia, will join to help the government. I fear that, very soon, the whole of Europe is going to slide into a war even more bloody than the one twenty years ago. If this happens, there is a very real danger that it will spread around the whole world. America and Japan might be drawn in. Millions of people will be killed, or maimed, or made home-less. If there is a chance to stop the madness, it must be done now, before the nightmare has properly begun. People at home need to know what is going on. Not just what the press and the government tells them, but what it all means to the average worker. I am here and I have a responsibility to find out all I can and take word back to Canada."

"But," said Ted, "if it is a war against fascism, shouldn't Canada be involved? You are always saying that people like Arcand have to be stopped."

"Yes, but not through violence. All wars, even those fought for a just cause, end up being fought for the benefit of the rich while the poor do all the dying." Will paused and looked at his son. "But you do have a point. If it comes to a world war and Canada is drawn in, then obviously she must be on the side of the greatest right. There are many fascists in Canada who support Hitler."

"Henry Thomas for one," Ted interrupted.

"Yes," Will agreed smiling, "Henry and his dad are typical of the sort. They're afraid of change. They think, and quite rightly, that socialism means change, and they think someone like Hitler is the way to prevent that change. What they don't see are the people tortured in the prison dungeons or left to rot in the concentration camps. They don't think they will ever hear the terrifying knock on the door at two in the morning or the shouts telling them to get into a truck that is going to whisk them off to God knows where. People like that aren't evil, just ignorant.

"Anyway, there are quite a number of these people in Canada and they will try as hard as they can to sabotage anything Canada does to stop Hitler and Mussolini. That's another reason I must go to Spain. To oppose these people we need information—information I can get.

"You asked me once how what I do at home can help someone in Germany, and my answer was very general. This is not. Perhaps what I discover here will help all those who are locked up and beaten by the Gestapo and the SS."

Ted sat in silence for a moment with only the gurgling of

the fountain and the occasional click of the old men's bowls to disturb him. He was still disappointed, but he was also proud of what Will was trying to do. He was giving up his holiday and the good time he was having to try and help others.

"How long will you be gone?" Ted asked quietly.

"Not too long," Will smiled and put his arm round his son's shoulder. "I got a name from the organization in Paris, Rafael Martinez. He is in something called POUM, which is very popular in Barcelona, so he should have an idea of what's going on. Just three or four days, a week at most, should be enough to collect some information and see a little for myself. If you and Mom go back to England, I'll contact you at the place we stayed in London. And, you can still do lots of fun things while you're waiting for me. After I get there, we might still have time to take a trip somewhere— maybe a few days in Scotland—before we catch the boat.

"It's important, Ted, not just for me, but for many other people and, perhaps, for the world you will grow up in. I'd like your support, and I need your help to make sure that Catherine goes on enjoying herself until I get back. Can you do that for me?"

Ted nodded slowly.

"I'll try," he said, "but be careful."

It was Will's turn to nod.

"Thanks," he said, reaching over and ruffling the hair on the back of Ted's head. Ted flinched involuntarily, but Will didn't seem to notice. "It'll be dark soon. Let's get back and get organized. We've still got a couple of days before my train leaves."

Sunday, July 19
to
Tuesday, July 21, 1936

⁘───────────⁘

The days before Will's departure were very tense. Mixed news kept coming from Spain. On Sunday Burgos, Valladolid and Salamanca fell to the rebels, but the revolt was crushed in Barcelona.

On Monday, the list of lost cities continued to grow as Cádiz, Oviedo and La Coruña were added, but again there was good news. Workers in Madrid stormed the Montaña Barracks and stopped the insurrection there. With the arms they had found, they were marching out to secure the nearby towns of Toledo and Guadalajara for the Republic. The French government announced it would sell Spain planes and small arms. This French assistance, combined with the news that the rebels were sending representatives to Italy and Germany to ask for help, further convinced Will that the world was on the verge of war.

By Tuesday morning, the rebels controlled about one third of Spain in two separate areas. Against the backdrop of these events, and of Will's rapidly approaching departure, it was impossible for the Ryans to pretend they were still on holiday. To make matters worse, posters announcing a large communist rally in support of the Spanish government on Tuesday afternoon began appearing all over town. The train to Paris did not leave until midnight on Tuesday. Will tried to persuade Ted and Catherine not to come to the station to see him off. They would be much safer, he said, staying indoors at the guest house until it was time for them to catch the Paris express. But both Ted and his mother were adamant—they were coming to the station to say goodbye. Eventually, Will gave in.

The journey to the railway station wasn't too bad. The rally hadn't begun, but crowds were already milling around waving flags and shouting. Ted watched nervously as several scuffles broke out. Uniformed police were everywhere. Fortunately, the family left their hotel early enough that, despite delays negotiating the crowd, they arrived in plenty of time for the train.

Tuesday, July 21, 1936
Afternoon

⌒⌒──────────⌒⌒

The maroon carriages lay alongside the platform like a sleeping serpent. Up ahead, white clouds of steam belched and hissed from the engine. Doors stood open and people everywhere were busily loading suitcases. Most of the passengers had dark hair and faces creased with worried expressions. Ted assumed they were Spaniards going home to find out what was happening in their war-torn country. Will, tall, thin and with his mop of straw-colored hair, seemed out of place. A tinny voice on the loudspeaker announced the imminent departure of the Barcelona train. It was almost time to say good-bye.

"I guess I'd better get settled," Will said, pushing his battered case through an open carriage window onto a vacant seat. "Looks like it's going to be crowded, so we'll probably be held up for hours at the border."

Will turned and embraced Catherine.

"Be careful going home," he said, holding her at arms length so he could look into her face. "I didn't like the look of the crowd on the way here. Stay indoors until it's time to go for the Paris train. I've wired Jean so he will meet you tomorrow morning and make sure you catch the boat for London. As soon as I can I'll contact you and let you know how things are going."

The pair stood still amongst the swirling mass of humanity. Then they embraced again and kissed.

Turning to Ted, Will put a hand on his son's shoulder. Ted was never going to be as tall as his father. He had known that for a long time, but now he felt dwarfed by the man before him. He had to fight back tears of sadness and pride.

"Remember what we talked about at the fountain?" Ted nodded. "Well, don't forget. Look after your mom, okay? I'll be back as soon as I can. A week at the most, I promise."

Will winked at his son, but spoiled the moment by ruffling Ted's hair. Then he was gone. Almost instantly, it seemed to Ted, he had turned and stepped through the open carriage door. Ted and his mom stood silently as Will fought his way to his compartment and stood looking at them through the open window.

"Take care," he shouted as the carriage lurched awkwardly and began its journey south. The crowd moved down the platform as if sucked along by the movement of the train. At first it kept up, but, as the carriages gathered speed, the people began began to fall back. Ted stopped to watch the familiar figure waving out of the window. He remained motionless until the curve of the track took his father out of sight. He didn't wave back.

Turning to his mother, Ted saw tears streaming down her face. He pulled a handkerchief out of his pocket, and offered the grubby cloth to her. His mom looked at him, smiled, took the rag and began dabbing her cheeks.

"Come on," said Ted, taking his mother's arm and feeling very adult, "Dad was right, we should be getting back as quickly as we can."

Slowly the pair made their way along the platform and out into the afternoon sun.

The crowds in the streets were even thicker now, and Ted and his mother had to force their way through. Everyone seemed to be shouting or singing. Occasionally, Ted caught the refrain of the communist *International*, but mostly the shouts just blended into an unintelligible mass.

Ted had intended to bypass the main square where the rally was planned, but in the crush and chaos he became disoriented. After about twenty minutes of battling the crowd, he found himself in a narrow street leading to an open area packed with people waving flags and banners. On the far side, a wooden platform stood beneath a huge red banner which proclaimed *"VIVA L'ESPAGNE LIBRE."* A man with a megaphone was on the platform addressing the crowd, but Ted doubted if anyone could hear what he was saying.

Not relishing the prospect of fighting through the mass of humanity in front of them, Ted led his mother back down the street. After about a block, they passed an alley that was empty apart from a canvas-covered delivery truck sitting at the far end.

The going was much easier in the alley, and the pair soon drew level with the truck. Its engine was idling with a low grumbling noise and a uniformed policeman was leaning casually against the front fender smoking and talking with the driver. He glanced up as Ted and his mother approached.

Ted felt uneasy. What was a delivery truck doing here with its engine running? No one in their right mind would be delivering anything this afternoon. As Ted and his mother arrived level with the tailgate, a canvas flap at the back lifted and a face peered out. The eyes were dark and cold and they met Ted's for only the briefest of moments, but it was long enough to send a shiver down the boy's spine. This was no delivery truck. It was filled with men. Men in black shirts. The kinds of men Will had told him about.

Holding his mother's arm tighter, Ted hurried past. The policeman watched them suspiciously, not acknowledging Ted's nod. Ted felt eyes boring into his back as they walked towards the next street and its welcoming riot of people. They didn't make it. Piercing whistles sounded from all directions. Ted glanced over his shoulder to see men scrambling out of the truck and running down the alley towards him. Each held a long, heavy club in one hand.

"Run," he shouted, pulling his mother's arm.

In a few steps they were in the crowd. Almost immediately the black-shirted men from the truck charged into the street and began clubbing people indiscriminately. Men, women and children screamed and ran in all directions. Barging through the mêlée, Ted led his mother towards the square. The scene there was even worse. The whistles had obviously been a signal and groups of armed men were attacking the rally from all sides. One black shirt was on the wooden platform hauling down the banner, while two others enthusiastically beat the man with the megaphone. All over the square, clubs were rising and falling. The chaos was indescribable.

Ted was paralyzed. All the way from the station he had felt important and in charge, taking over the care of his mother now that Will was gone. Now he didn't know what to do. All courses of action seemed equally dangerous.

"Come on, Ted," he felt his mother's arm around his shoulder urging him forward, "this way looks a bit more open."

Pushing through the bodies, the pair headed towards the quietest corner of the square. They had almost made it, when a huge bull of a man blocked the way. The man wasn't in uniform, but he was a frightful sight nonetheless. He was over six feet tall and was dressed in filthy work clothes which were patched apparently at random. His face was contorted in pain. Rivulets of blood coursed down from his hair, across his rough face and disappeared under his grubby collar. His

eyes gazed at Ted but they were empty and unfocused.

With an incoherent grunt, the monster lunged forward. Before Ted could react, the man's knee came up, catching him below the ribs and knocking the wind out of him. Ted grunted and fell to the ground. His head smashed into the cobblestones with a searing pain.

Ted lay gasping like a stranded fish. The noise of the square disappeared behind the ringing in his ears. The world slowed down. The legs around him seemed to move as if they were wading through molasses. Ted was fascinated by the variety of the legs. Some were short and stubby, others so thin and stick-like that he felt he could reach out and snap them like dry twigs. One pair in particular caught his befuddled attention. They were dressed in calf-length black boots which gleamed with a mirrored shine.

"Wish I had a pair of boots like that," Ted mused.

Then he saw his mother. She too had been pushed aside by the brute. Her hair was disheveled and she had lost her purse, but she was struggling to get back to him.

"It's okay," Ted wanted to shout, "I'm just lying here looking at the boots."

But no sound came out of his mouth. His lungs and throat were on fire and black spots were swimming in front of his eyes. Ted's mother leaned over him. Her lips were moving silently. There was someone behind her.

"Look out!" the words were like jello slowly solidifying

in Ted's brain. He was helpless. The owner of the shiny black boots was standing behind his mother with his club raised. The last two things Ted remembered were the sickening crack of the club on his mother's skull and the soft weight of her body landing across his legs. Then all the black spots coagulated and he passed out.

Tuesday, July 21, 1936
Evening

In one sense, Catherine was lucky—she had a bed. Even now, hours after the riot, there were still people in the hospital corridors. But, Ted reflected ruefully, both the bed and the swiftness with which his mother had been put in it were probably indicators of how badly hurt she was. It was late evening and she had not yet regained consciousness. In the fading light, she lay silent and still. Strands of brown hair stuck out awkwardly from beneath the white bandage covering most of her head. She lay on her back, eyes closed and mouth slightly open as if she were simply taking a nap. She had been like this for hours. The regular, shallow rise and fall of the sheets over her chest had not changed despite all the poking and prodding by doctors.

There had been mumbled consultations, too, but Ted had understood none of them and no one around spoke English. The only exception had been the young man Ted had found crouched over his mother when he had come to in the square. By then the fighting had stopped and people were busy attending to the injured. Ted's memory had come back slowly through the waves of pain emanating from the base of his skull. The stranger had spoken first.

"Bonjour. Comment ça va?"

"I'm sorry," Ted's tongue felt too big for his mouth and his words sounded slurred, "I don't understand. I don't speak French."

"Ah. You are American?" The man's voice was heavily accented, but Ted had little trouble understanding him.

"No," Ted replied, "Canadian. How is my mother?"

Ted was sitting up now, but he didn't want to move any further because that would disturb his mother's still form.

"Your mother," the stranger nodded, "she is not good." He hesitated for a moment, *"les cochons*...the pigs, they hit her very hard. I think we should go to the hospital. How are you?"

"I'm okay," Ted lied. His head hurt unbearably, which made speech and movement a terrible effort. But he didn't think there was anything seriously wrong. He was much more worried about his mother.

"Will she be all right?" he asked, groggily.

"I think yes," the young man replied as he rose and waved to some men carrying a stretcher through the chaos of the square.

The rest of the afternoon had been a painful, worried confusion of bumpy, overcrowded ambulances and clusters of unintelligible doctors. The hospital had been a scene of utter pandemonium—men and women sprawled wherever there was floor space. Most had blood on them and many held bloody rags to their heads. Doctors and nurses hurried up and down the hallways attending to the worst cases. The evening was much quieter, at least in the wards, but Ted was no closer to knowing how his mother was. He fervently wished Will was here. Will would know what to do.

Ted's musings were interrupted by a shadow falling across the bed. He looked up to see the man from the square smiling down at him. The man was dressed in a crumpled suit and an open-necked white shirt. Now that Ted had a chance to look at him, he appeared little older than Ted himself.

"Bonjour," he said holding out his hand. "We had no chance for introductions today. My name is Bernard. I am a medical student here at the hospital."

"How do you do," said Ted rising rather stiffly. "My name's Ted. Thank you for our help in the square."

"Oh," Bernard shrugged, *"de rien.* How do you feel now?"

"I'm fine My head hurts a bit, but that's all. But my mother, she hasn't woken up yet."

"Oui," Bernard glanced over at the still figure. "The doctors say she has had a severe blow to the head." He hesitated, then looked back at Ted. "It may be some time before she wakes up," he said slowly.

"But she *will* wake up?" Ted felt a chill spreading down

his spine. "Won't she?"

Bernard held Ted's gaze with his own. "She has been hit very hard. The skull is not broken and there is no bleeding, but we cannot look inside. She may wake up in a few hours, or days, or…"

"Never," Ted interrupted as he slumped back into his chair and gazed at the form on the bed. He had never felt so worried and alone. In one day he had lost both parents and been dumped in a situation where he felt totally helpless. His father had gone off to war, his mother was in a coma, he had hardly any money, couldn't speak the language and the nearest Canadian consul was a day's journey away in Paris. What if his mother didn't wake up? How long would they stay here? How would they get back to Canada? How could he possibly pay for the hospital?

It was all overwhelming. But even worse was the guilt Ted felt. Not guilt at his inability to protect his mother, he knew there was very little he could have done in the madness of the square, it was guilt because he couldn't cry. All afternoon, Ted had wondered what would happen if his mother never woke up, or if the slow rise and fall of the sheet suddenly stopped. These had been terrifying thoughts, but Ted's eyes had stayed dry. And that made him feel horribly guilty. Surely any normal boy would cry for his mother if she was this sick. What was wrong with him?

"Your father, he is in Canada?" Bernard's voice interrupted Ted's thoughts.

"No," Ted replied, "he is in Spain. We were returning from seeing him off on the train to Barcelona when we got caught in the riot."

Ted caught Bernard looking at him very intently.

"Why did he go to Spain?" he asked slowly.

"To find out what was going on," Ted answered. "He is afraid what is happening in Spain is the beginning of a much bigger war. He wants to be able to tell the people back in Canada what is happening."

"He is a communist then, your father?"

"No, he is a socialist." Ted had little idea what the difference was, but he knew it was important to Will.

"Yes," said Bernard nodding, "there are many socialists with broken heads in here today. The black shirts were very busy this afternoon."

"Why didn't the police stop them?" Ted was remembering the policeman standing smoking by the truck full of armed thugs.

"Ha," Bernard laughed bitterly, "the police are as bad as the fascists. They stand by and laugh as communists are beaten, and protect the thugs who do the beating. It is not a good time to be a worker. Fortunately, today, no one was killed."

Ted caught Bernard's quick glance over at his mother's still form before he continued.

"What will you do?"

It was a question Ted had been thinking about. He had enough money in loose change for a couple of meals, and his passport which he always kept in his back pocket, but that was all. He had a room for the night which was paid for but a train ticket was out of the question. Even if his mother was well enough to travel, the train reservations, the contact names and addresses in Paris and London, and the remainder of their money were all in her purse, and Ted hadn't seen that since the square. It certainly wasn't here at the hospital. Ted had searched around, and asked as best he could, but his questions had only been met with infuriating shrugs.

"I don't know," he said helplessly.

"Your father," continued Bernard trying a different approach, "he comes back here."

"No," Ted replied automatically, "he is going to meet us in London." Then a new and frightening thought struck him. "If Mom doesn't wake up, I don't know the name or address of the contact in London. I only know we were supposed to meet a man called Jean in Paris on the way. I have no way of getting there or getting a message to him. My dad will arrive in London in a week and, if Mom's still unconscious, we won't be there. He will have no way of knowing where we are—whether we are in Paris, here, back in Canada, or anywhere else. Even if I can contact the Canadian consul, we still have no way of contacting Dad in London. What am I going to do?"

Now Ted really felt cast adrift. Until Catherine woke up, he couldn't see any way the family could be reunited. Will and Ted were separated and alone in the vast, alien complexity of Europe.

"Do you know where in Barcelona your father went?" Throughout Ted's explanation, Bernard had been watching him closely.

"Only a name," Ted searched his memory, "Rafael something, Martinez, I think. He is in something called the P...O...U...M. That's not much to go on."

"But it might be enough. The POUM is a workers' organization. Rafael Martinez should be easy enough to find through them and he might know where your father is."

A possibility was opening before Ted. If he could get to Barcelona quickly, he might be able to catch Will and bring him back. Then the family would be reunited.

"But I can't leave Mom." Ted looked over at the pale face on the pillow. "In any case, I don't have the money for a train ticket."

"Yes," agreed Bernard, "it is difficult. But she may remain this way for some time. She will be well looked after here, I would see to it myself. I know many of the doctors. Your lack of money is a bigger problem, but I am sure something could be worked out. The train ticket need not bother you, there are many ways to go to Spain from here— we are close to the border. Just this evening, I was with some friends who are planning to drive to Barcelona to see what is going on. I am sure they would be happy to take you along if you wish. With luck you could find your father and be back in two or three days.

"But we are looking on the black side. Most probably your mother will wake in the night with nothing more than a sore head. I would suggest you go back to your room and get some sleep. I have a car, I can give you a lift. In the morning, you will probably find her sitting up enjoying croissants and coffee. I will drop by tomorrow to see how you both are."

On the drive back through the dark streets Ted realized how weary he was. His head still hurt and every muscle in his body felt like it had been beaten. Despite this exhaustion, he found that sleep would not come.

For most of the night, Ted tossed and turned, wondering what to do and worrying about his family. Finally, just as the sun was rising, he dropped off into a fitful sleep amidst dreams of being lost and alone.

Wednesday, July 22, 1936

When morning finally arrived, Ted hurriedly packed his few things in a tattered bag. He stuffed Catherine's belongings in her suitcase and left it with the caretaker. He walked to the hospital in a turmoil of hope and fear—hope that his mother would be sitting up in bed to greet him, and fear that the bed would be empty.

Neither was the case. Ted's mother was exactly the same as the evening before, and she remained unconscious all day. At first Ted was sad, miserable, upset, confused, but his mother's unchanging body lying between the white sheets seemed so peaceful and content that he felt a sort of tranquility stealing over him. Doctors came and went, discussing things amongst themselves and shrugging in their particularly French way when Ted tried to talk to them, but Catherine didn't seem to mind. To Ted she seemed to be smiling, and he relaxed, despite the bustle of the hospital ward around him. Ted was tired and hungry, but he dared not leave to get some food in case Bernard came to translate what the doctors were saying. Eventually, towards evening, he dozed off, dreaming that he was still awake.

As he watched his mother's immobile face, she slowly sat

up and turned to face him.

"Why do you look so sad?" she asked.

"Because you are sick and Dad is not here," he replied.

"I am not sick, I am just very tired. I need to rest. Where is your father?"

"He's in Spain," said Ted.

"Oh," Catherine continued distractedly, "I had so wished he were here." Her smile faded and slowly she lay back on the bed.

Ted awoke with a start, just in time to prevent himself from falling out of the chair. He ached all over and felt as if someone had painted fur over his tongue while he slept.

"Hello," Ted looked up to see Bernard's familiar face watching him from across the bed. "You were tired, perhaps you did not sleep well last night?"

"No," said Ted thickly. "You should have woken me."

Bernard shrugged.

"Have you talked to the doctors?" Ted continued. "How is my mother?"

"There is no change. Her heart is strong. Except for the bump on the head, there is nothing obviously wrong with her," Bernard hesitated and glanced at the pale form. "It is strange though. Have you noticed?"

"What?" Ted's voice was tinged with anxiety.

"Her face," continued Bernard, "looks so sad. Yesterday I could have sworn she was smiling."

Ted stood and bent over the bed. Bernard was right, the smile had faded. He remembered his dream.

"Bernard," he said, standing up, "yesterday you mentioned some friends who might be able to take me to Barcelona."

"Yes, they plan to leave tomorrow morning."

"Do you think they would still take me?"

"I am sure," Bernard replied. "I think perhaps they will also give you a bed for the night," he added, glancing at Ted's bag by the foot of the bed. "Let us go and see them and, on the way, we can find something to eat, yes? You look as if you could use a good meal."

Ted nodded. Leaning over the bed, he whispered, "Mom, I'm going to find Will. I'll only be gone a couple of days and Bernard and the doctors will look after you here. The family will soon be back together again."

Kissing his mother on the cheek, Ted turned, picked up his bag and followed Bernard out of the ward.

Thursday, July 23, 1936
Morning

The old Ford station wagon rattled and bumped its way through the rocky, dry landscape of northern Spain. The heat was stifling and was intensified by the eternal dust clouds that followed the vehicle everywhere. No matter how uncomfortably the passengers sweated with the windows rolled tightly shut, dust always managed to find a way into the car. Ted was stuffed in the back, amidst bedrolls, bags of clothes and boxes of canned food. He felt like a limp rag. His clothes were soaked in sweat; his eyes, dry and irritated. Even the occasional, distant, inviting blue of the Mediterranean Sea served only to emphasize his discomfort.

Ted had fashioned a seat as best he could out of the supplies, but there was limited space to work with. Each bump in the road jarred his spine or banged his head on the roof. "Lucky I don't get car sick," Ted thought ruefully as he gazed with envy at the four young Frenchmen seated so comfortably in the front. Not that they were deliberately trying to make him uncomfortable. There was no alternative to the present arrangement—Ted was the only one of the five travelers small enough to fit in the crowded back, and Pierre, the driver, stopped frequently to allow Ted to stretch his aching joints.

The party had left Perpignan at first light and crossed into Spain at Port-Bou, a minor crossing post with a reputation for being more relaxed than the main posts at Le Perthus or Bourg-Madame. Even so, the party had anticipated problems. On the French side, the process had turned out to be ridiculously easy. With nothing more than a cursory examination of passports, they had been waved through. One of the French officials had even given the clenched fist salute of the socialists as they passed the barrier.

The Spanish guards were a different matter. They forced the five companions out of the car, not an easy feat for Ted, and examined their documents suspiciously. Each Spaniard carried a rifle over his shoulder. Their faces were thin and swarthy, with heavy black eyebrows and unshaven cheeks. Ted could not imagine those faces smiling and was beginning to doubt the wisdom of his decision to come to Spain. However, one of Ted's companions was a communist and the minute he handed over his party membership card, the tone of the meeting changed dramatically. The impassive, stern faces of moments before opened into a forest of smiles. Bottles of harsh-tasting red wine were produced and there was a flurry of back-slapping and raised fists. Loaves of bread and rolls of coarse sausage were thrust upon them before they were allowed, amidst much shouting, to proceed.

The only traffic on the back roads they traveled was the occasional farmer leading a donkey and, once, an antiquated tractor pulling an immense threshing machine. The landscape looked deserted. Even the small villages they passed through appeared abandoned. Though only a few hours away from the lush gardens of Perpignan, Spain seemed like a completely different world. Despite an occasional field of grain, most hillsides around the villages were covered with gnarled olive trees or rows of stunted grape vines. The walls of the villages themselves were more like natural outgrowths of the earth than the work of the people who inhabited them.

What surprised Ted most was the lack of any sign of the turmoil he had been told about. Many of the village walls had slogans painted on them and, although Ted understood little of what he saw, he did recognize *revolución,* *libertad,* and *collectivitzado.* The letters CNT-FAI which Ted assumed were the initials of some worker's organization or other—were also prominent. Apart from the slogans, however, life seemed to go on unaffected.

As Ted mused on the strangeness of his situation, the car screeched to a halt, throwing the unprepared boy painfully against a box of canned food. Peering out the windshield, Ted could make out the shape of a rough barricade across the road. He groaned at the sight of several figures with rifles approaching the car. Stiffly, he dragged himself over the back seat and out the door after his French companions. There were six figures standing in a semi-circle regarding the party. Only two actually had rifles. A third held a heavy, ugly revolver pointed at the ground in front of him. The remaining trio carried a pitchfork and two vicious-looking scythes. All were dressed in a semi-uniform of dark blue overalls on which was stitched a square divided into two triangles—one red, one black. Ted was surprised to see that two of the figures were girls, little older than himself. One of the men with a rifle stepped forward.

"Quiénes son ustedes?" he asked, raising his rifle uncomfortably close to Ted's stomach.

Pierre, who spoke some Spanish, replied. A halting conversation ensued while Ted nervously watched the wavering end of the gun. At last, after much document examination, many declarations of loyalty to *'la revolución'* and the *'Frente Popular,'* and the passing around of a wineskin, they were allowed through. The town behind the barricade was the largest they had seen. Several people were about and watched curiously as the car drove past. Here and there, some windows and doors were broken and the small church on the main square was blackened and deserted. Ted was glad when they left the narrow streets and headed back onto the dusty open roads.

A pattern was established at the roadblocks scattered randomly along the route. At first there was suspicion, much waving of weapons and serious questioning. Once credentials were established, this gave way to declarations of common cause, shouts of solidarity and the almost magical production of food and wine. At one stop, a guard even grabbed a nearby paintbrush and rudely scrawled CNT-FAI in white on the hood and sides of the station wagon. This eased their journey, but it was still mid-afternoon before they had completed the 200 kilometers to Barcelona's sprawling suburbs.

Thursday, July 23, 1936
Afternoon

After a hectic drive through winding Barcelona streets crowded with trucks, cars and horse-drawn carts, the travelers arrived at a wide square which still sported signs of the recent street fighting. One of the side streets was blocked with a hastily erected barricade of cobblestones, broken wagons and, oddly, a luxuriously upholstered armchair perched atop the untidy pile in solitary splendour. To Ted's horror, at one side of the barricade, a group of men were working hard to extricate the body of a large horse. On the opposite side of the square, the burned-out skeleton of a car lay on its side. Many of the surrounding walls were chipped by what Ted assumed were bullet holes. But it was the people who most held his attention. The square was crowded with men and women going about their afternoon business. They were mostly dressed in drab civilian working clothes or blue overalls and many wore red and black scarves around their necks. The occasional girl in a bright summer dress added a welcome splash of color. Couples strolled arm-in-arm and groups of men stood engrossed in animated discussions. Set against a backdrop of walls covered with revolutionary slogans and posters, the scene had a vibrance which struck Ted immediately. Something different, something outside Ted's experience was going on.

Two elements contributed strongly to Ted's initial impression. Firstly, amongst the dozens of men milling around, there was not one in a suit or even a tie; all were workers. Secondly, a good half of the men carried rifles slung casually over their right shoulder. Ted had never seen so many weapons, yet there was no sense of threat. Everyone appeared happy. The scene looked like a carnival rather than a city in the midst of a revolution.

Pierre worked the car over to an imposing edifice with the words "Hotel Colon" across its front in huge letters. Below, a banner was strung bearing the letters PSUC. Pierre led Ted over to the door where several armed men stood on the steps.

"*Salud,*" he began, "*Dónde está el POUM, por favor?*"

The men smiled at Pierre's accent and pointed down a wide boulevard which ran from one corner of the square.

Pierre handed Ted a tattered piece of paper with his address on it and shook his hand.

"Good luck," he said, using his only two words of English.

"*Merci,*" replied Ted as he set off through the crowd.

Now that he was amongst the people, the carnival atmosphere was more intense. The boulevard, Ramblas, was wide and lined with trees on both sides and along the center meridian. Outside cafés, customers drank coffee and wine, their weapons propped handily against their tables. Red and black flags hung from balconies and windows; walls were plastered with garish posters showing men and women with clenched fists straining towards the sky. All the shops and cafés had painted signs with *"collectivitzado"* on them.

Ted knew what that meant. Will had told him about the anarchists who wanted to do away with all structure and turn business and industry into collectives run by the workers. All profits would be shared equally. To accomplish this, the workers were prepared to kill all the owners and bosses. Ted wondered if this explained why he could see no one in a suit and tie.

A wide variety of cars, some obviously expropriated from rich owners, drove aimlessly along the street. Each vehicle was painted crudely with the initials of a workers' organization: CNT-FAI; UGT; PSUC; and, Ted was gratified to see, POUM. Some cars were covered with all the initials, as if their new owners wanted to emphasize their loyalty to the revolution as a whole. Armed men hung out the automobile windows or stood on the running boards shouting and waving their rifles.

Ted kept on walking, desperately trying to take in all the new and dramatic impressions crowding in on him. Suddenly, he noticed a commotion ahead. People were running to the curb, waving and cheering. Ted pushed his way through the crowd and saw a group of about a hundred figures marching down the street. They were dressed in civilian clothes, although some wore the blue overalls Ted had seen in the northern villages. All carried rifles and most had belts around their waists and bandoliers of ammunition across their chests. The only standardized pieces of uniform were rope sandals, red and black scarves around the throat, and caps, peaked fore and aft. As the marchers drew closer, Ted was amazed to see that many were women. The crowd cheered and shouted and waved clenched fists. Red and black flags fluttered above the marchers, who carried a huge poster of a heavy-set man in a leather coat. He seemed to peer out of the placard from beneath a pair of dark eyebrows with a look that said, "No one will stop me!"

Wild enthusiasm swept along the sidewalk as the marchers passed by. *"Anarchistas,"* the crowd shouted, "Durruti, Durruti."

Ted was overwhelmed. The marchers, the shouting, and the surging crowds were exciting, yet he understood almost nothing about what was happening. Ted had not exchanged more than two words with anyone all day. This was going to be more difficult than he thought. Still he had to remain focused, find Rafael Martinez, and through him, Will. Then he could get back to his mother. With a weary shrug, Ted turned and pushed his way through the crowd to the wide sidewalk. Almost immediately he spotted what he was looking for. It was a large building with balconies below every window and ornate, carved stonework all over. Above the door was a wide banner with the words *Partido Obrero Unificación Marxista.*

Almost gratefully, Ted ran up the steps. Inside was a large hall backed by a sweeping flight of marble stairs. People milled around to no obvious purpose. Grabbing the nearest person, Ted asked, "Rafael Martinez?" He received a string of unintelligible Spanish in reply and an arm pointing up the stairs and to the left.

Ted took the steps two at a time and found himself in a long corridor with rooms on both sides. All the doors were open and men with rifles were going in and out. Ted repeated his question and was led down the hall to a large room. Five desks were scattered randomly around the room beneath an incredibly ornate crystal chandelier. Each desk was piled high with paper, and the room was filled with the busy clack of typewriters. Ted's guide led him over to a desk which seemed less cluttered than the others. An empty chair stood beside it. Pointing at the middle-aged man behind the desk, he said, "*Camarada* Martinez," and left.

The man behind the desk looked up. He had a round face without the heavy dark eyebrows and unshaven chin that Ted was coming to expect in the Spaniards he met. *"Salud,"* he said.

"I'm sorry, I don't speak Spanish," Ted apologized. "Are you Rafael Martinez?"

"Yes," replied the man, standing up and switching effortlessly to English. "That is my name. How may I help you?"

The relief at hearing a language he could understand flooded over Ted and the whole story of the last few days poured out.

Rafael Martinez listened patiently, nodding encouragement occasionally. When Ted finally ran out of steam, he shook his head in sympathy.

"You have certainly had quite an adventure. It is a brave thing you are doing. Yes, I met your father. He was here yesterday."

"Where is he now?" Ted interrupted, looking around as if he expected to see Will standing in a corner of the room. "Can I go to him?"

Rafael Martinez sat down and indicated the empty chair to Ted.

"Unfortunately," he began, clasping his hands under his chin, "there is a problem. Your father is no longer here."

"Where has he gone?" Ted jumped up from his chair almost as soon as he had sat in it. "Where is he now?"

"Please sit, I will tell you what happened. Your father was very interested in our struggle and our revolution. We talked much yesterday of the collectivization that is going on in the city and surrounding countryside. Will was very interested in everything I could show him. He did not know that we are having a revolution. The workers have taken over everything from the trams to the clothing factories. The bosses and owners have either fled to the fascists or are in hiding. Your father wanted to see everything, particularly what is happening in the country.

"You come from a fruit-growing area in Canada, I believe? Well, no matter. One of our militias was leaving for Aragon; there is fighting in the hills around Huesca and Zaragoza. I offered Will the chance to accompany our men and observe. He jumped at the opportunity, I think, because he wanted to see much quickly and get back to you and your mother as soon as possible. Your father left this morning."

Ted slumped down crestfallen. So close. If he had arrived yesterday he would probably have found Will sitting at this very desk. They would already be united and on their way back. But it had not been possible. Yesterday Ted hadn't known if his mother would wake up or not and, anyway, he could not have gotten a ride. Ted would have to go on alone.

"Where exactly is my father and how can I get there?"

"First things first," Martinez gazed at Ted thoughtfully. "You cannot leave before tomorrow and I must make inquiries to see if it is possible. Perhaps something to eat while you wait? My daughter would be happy to help you. She gets little chance to practice her English these days."

Martinez turned to an open door which Ted assumed led

to a side room, and shouted "Dolores."

In a moment a girl about Ted's age appeared in the doorway. She was dressed in a white cotton blouse with the sleeves rolled up past her elbows, and a shapeless pair of men's trousers. Around her neck, like a bright splash of blood, was knotted a deep red scarf. Her hair was shoulder length and tucked behind her ears. She was smiling and looked across the room at her father with a pair of the largest, darkest, brown eyes Ted had ever seen.

"*Si* Papa," she said brightly as she came into the room.

"My dear," Martinez's face softened visibly as his daughter approached. "I have found someone for you to speak English with. This young man is Ted. He is from Canada."

The girl turned her smile on Ted who hurriedly stood up.

"*Hola* Ted," she said, extending her hand, "I am exceptionally pleased to make the acquaintance of you."

Flustered, as much by her awkward expression as by the eyes which were slowly turning his knees to butter, Ted mumbled, "Hello, pleased to meet you," and shook hands.

Thankfully, Martinez saved Ted from having to think of anything else to say. "Dolores, Ted is hungry. Perhaps you might accompany him to a café for some food while I see if I can find a way to help him rejoin his father?"

"Yes," she answered and her smile broadened as she looked down. Ted realized with horror that his hand, obeying some impulse of its own, had not yet let go of hers. Hurriedly he withdrew it.

"Come Ted," said Dolores, turning to the main door, "let us find you some comestibles."

Realizing that there was indeed a hollow feeling deep in his stomach, Ted muttered, "Thank you," in Martinez's direction and followed Dolores into the crowded corridor.

Thursday, July 23, 1936
Evening

⚮━━━━━━━━⚮

The Café Moka was immediately beside POUM head-quarters. It was a warm summer's evening, even at the outside tables in the growing shadow of the building. The Ramblas was busier than ever with crowds of people strolling in the late sunshine. It was hard to imagine there was a war on and that, only days before, machine-gun bullets had torn along this very street.

Ted ate a huge plate of rich pork and tomato stew and was feeling almost human again. To his horror, Dolores had demolished a large plate of snails. They had eaten in silence, but, with a full stomach, Ted felt more like talking.

"Where did you learn to speak English?"

"I lived in England for two years. In the town of Cambridge," Dolores replied. "My father taught there. He is an…uhm…philosophist?"

"Philosopher," Ted corrected with a smile.

"*Si,*" his companion smiled back, "a philosopher. I learned, but I was little and have not the chance to practice as much as I would wish. But I read. Mr. Dickens is my best author. *Oliver Twist* is my favorite." The smile broadened to reveal a row of strikingly white teeth. "You have read it?"

"No," Ted found himself smiling back. "Not that one, but I have read *A Christmas Carol*. I enjoyed that."

"Hah," Dolores shook her head dismissively, "it is too much bourgeois. Scrooge should give all his money away, not just a little on festivals. All capitalists are misers, no?"

"I don't know." Ted felt unprepared for the question. "I suppose some are."

"I think all. But we have no capitalists left now in Spain, only workers and fascists."

"What happened to them?" Ted asked. "Did the anarchists kill them?"

"Some," she said matter-of-factly. "The rest ran away or are hiding in their houses."

Dolores was interrupted by a man squeezing past her chair. His rifle butt banged against the edge of the table, grazing her arm.

"Excusa, camarada."

"Why are there so many guns around?" Ted asked, "I had heard that the fighting was over."

Dolores's laugh sounded to Ted like tiny silver bells falling over a waterfall. "In Barcelona the fighting is never over. Every year there is a riot and people go behind the barricades. It is said that they should number the cobblestones to make it easier to replace them afterwards."

Dolores became more serious. "But yes, a few days ago there was much fighting. The workers were given guns because only they could defend us. Many were killed. Some say hundreds. Now the workers must be all things: policemen, *guardia*, soldiers, everything. And many are militia. The fascists are advancing from Zaragoza. We must stop them. We must build an army. We are fighting a war and having a revolution at the same time. It is not easy. I wish to go and fight with the militia, but my father, he is not so happy that I do that. Will Canada help us?"

"I don't know," Ted replied. "That is why Will, my father, came down here. We were on holiday in France and he came down to find out what was happening so he could tell people back in Canada." Ted sighed. Canada seemed very far away at this moment. An image of his mother lying immobile on her hospital bed flooded over him. "My mother was hurt in a riot and I have come to find my father and take him back. She is very sick."

"I am sorry," Dolores looked down at the table. "My mother died two years ago."

"I'm sorry," Ted mumbled. For a moment he thought Dolores was going to cry, but when she looked up Ted saw anger not sorrow in her eyes.

"My mother was killed," Dolores explained quietly, "murdered by the fascists. She was always more of a…," Dolores paused and searched for the right word, "a *político* than my father. He was happy teaching at the university and talking of these people who have been dead for many years: Descartes and Spinoza. My father used to say to my mother when she became excitable about an injustice by the police, 'Do not worry so much. It will all be the same in one hundred years.'

"'That is too long,' my mother would reply, 'we must make it different tomorrow.' She marched in parades, she helped striking workers, she went into the countryside with a traveling theatre group to present socialist ideas to those who could neither read nor write. When the miners revolted in Asturias in October 1934, my mother went to help. My father tried to stop her. He agreed with the revolt, but he is a watcher not a doer. My mother said, 'These may be the first shots of the revolution. I cannot stand by and watch something I have always fought for happen in my own country and not help.'

"But it was not her dream commencing. The revolt did not last long. The government was of the right at that time. It was the *Bienio Negro*—the two black years. They brought in the Moorish soldiers under General Franco and the *Guardia Civil* under the butcher Doval. We were told officially that mother was killed by a stray bullet in the fighting, but a comrade told us later that he had seen my mother with a group of miners being marched to prison, where many were deliberately shot by the soldiers.

"The news devastated my father. He gave up his position at the university and has worked for the POUM ever since. It is his way to answer my mother."

"Do you agree with him?"

"Sometimes, yes," the anger faded from Dolores's face. "My father is…how do you say…living in his mind?"

"An intellectual?" Ted suggested helpfully.

"*Si*, an intellectual. He thinks we should not have our revolution until we have defeated the army."

"And you don't?"

"No, because our revolution is already something that has happened. Nobody planned it and nobody can stop it now. The workers are in charge and everyone is happy—look."

Dolores waved her arm to indicate the crowds strolling on the street. Almost as if her gesture had triggered it, there was a loud crack and a long drawn out *zeeeeeee*, as a bullet ricocheted off the sidewalk. Instantly the scene changed. People threw themselves on the ground or ran for shelter. Those with weapons began firing wildly in all directions. The noise was deafening. Ted grabbed Dolores's arm and pulled her into the café doorway, more to get away from the return fire than from whoever was responsible for the first shot.

"What happened?" he asked breathlessly.

"I don't know." Dolores's eyes were wide with excitement. "Perhaps a fascist sniper, perhaps an accident. My compatriots are not very good shots and they are very excitable."

Already the firing was dying down. People were beginning to pick themselves up from the ground and look around.

"Let us go back and see if my father has found our way to the front."

The pair slipped quickly around the corner and into the POUM building. Ted's heart was pounding, not because of the shooting, but because Dolores had said "our way to the front" when she spoke about finding Will. Perhaps he wouldn't be lonely after all.

Rafael Martinez was halfway down the stairs on his way to check that they were all right.

"Hello, children," he said. "I am glad you are okay." As they walked back to his desk, he explained what he had found out.

"I made a few phone calls, a slow process now that the anarchists control the telephone exchange, but I think I have found a way to the front. There is an ambulance leaving early tomorrow for our unit and the driver has agreed to take Ted along. From the aid station it should be easy to find your father."

"I will accompany him." It was a statement, not a question. Martinez turned in mid-stride and regarded his daughter.

"Papa," Dolores continued, "Ted speaks no Spanish. How will he find himself around our militia without me?"

"I suppose, if I say no," Martinez said eventually, "you

will find a way to go without my permission?" Dolores smiled. "In any case, as you found out, you are just as likely to be shot at on the streets outside as you will be at the aid station." Martinez turned to Ted with a resigned air, "My daughter is very headstrong, like her mother." Turning again to Dolores, he continued, "But I will set some rules. The aid station is behind the front. You are to send a message to Ted's father from there informing him of your presence. Under no circumstances are you to leave the station. Do you understand?" Ted and Dolores both nodded.

"You must promise me this or I will not allow either of you to go."

"I promise," they said together.

"Good," Martinez continued. "now we must find you somewhere to sleep. I will not go home tonight, there is still much I have to do here. We have a boarding house for militia at the Hotel Falcon at the bottom of Ramblas. You will be able to get beds there. In any case, the ambulance is leaving from the Comite Local across the street, so you will be close. I will come down to see you off. Now go. Get some sleep. Be careful."

Martinez hugged his daughter and shook Ted's hand. In a few moments they were back on the street where there was not the slightest evidence that anything untoward had happened a few minutes before.

Friday, July 24, 1936
Morning

❧———————————☙

The ambulance ride reminded Ted of his trip to Barcelona. Every Spanish road seemed simply a generally agreed upon direction over the landscape where vehicles were forced to negotiate ruts and potholes deep enough to discourage the fainthearted. Their driver, a German who spoke little English and even less Spanish, was not daunted. With an abandon that put a tremendous strain on the vehicle and the nerves of its passengers, he took the straightest route, crashing through potholes as if they didn't exist. When he had to corner, he flung the wheel around, spraying dirt in all directions.

"He is a foreign volunteer who has fled from Hitler," explained Dolores, "but he will do well here. He drives like a Spaniard."

"Ja, like a Spaniard," the driver shouted proudly, "and I fight like a Spaniard, too. This is my country now." He banged the dashboard as the vehicle swung wildly around another corner.

"What about Germany?" Ted asked. "Isn't Germany your

country?"

"Germany kaput," the man exclaimed disdainfully. "Hitler will destroy it. I am socialist—union man—in Hamburg. One day the SD—the brownshirts—came. They arrest everyone. We all go to prison. Many are beaten. I was too. Some were killed, I think. Then we all go on truck to Dachau, a big camp near Berlin. All socialists and communists in Germany are there. There were many beatings and some deaths. The guards are very cruel. I was there eight months, then a group of us were put on a train and sent across the border to France. I think because my brother was in Paris and made much loud noise for me. Anyway, I have no papers. I cannot go back. I am stateless. Spain is my home now.

"Maybe there is much fighting here. Maybe we will win. Then maybe we will go and fight Hitler."

The driver laughed. He took both hands off the wheel in order to beat out the rhythm of a German drinking song.

Conversation was limited by the necessity to hang on for dear life and by the driver's cheerful propensity to spontaneously burst into song. Nevertheless, between choruses and corners, Ted managed to tell Dolores about his life in Canada, the trip to Vancouver, the "On-to-Ottawa" trek and Uncle Roger's fiery, unexpected death. Ted's story seemed bland compared to what Dolores was living through, but she listened attentively, and seemingly enthralled by his descriptions of the fruit orchards of the Okanagan Valley and the lakesides where Ted spent most of his summer days.

"In Spain we have no lakes," she said, "and our trees are only old twisted olives which are, I think, not very beautiful. I have heard of your maple syrup trees. I should like to acquaint myself with them."

Ted didn't have the heart to tell her there were no maple syrup trees in the Okanagan Valley—her enthusiasm was far too infectious.

In turn, Dolores told Ted about the Spanish workers' struggles against a repressive army and police, a corrupt Church and avaricious landlords.

"It is six years now since we ousted King Alfonso," she explained. "It has been a most difficult time, but we make progress. There has been land and education reform, but it does not make everyone happy. The Church and the landowners want nothing to change. The peasants want change too quickly. There is much conflict. Many deaths.

"The peasants in the countryside are no better than slaves, trodden down by the Church and *la Guardia*. If they complain, they are shot. That is why anarchism is the religion of the landless. It is their only hope for a better world. The peasants do not need the God of their landlords, so they have burned all the churches or turned them into storehouses. In some villages, the anarchists have done away with money altogether. People take what they need from the common wealth. They are creating a new world."

"Who is Durruti?" Ted asked, remembering the shouts as the militia passed him the day before.

"Buenaventura Durruti. He is a famous anarchist. In 1923, he and his friend, Francisco Ascaso, murdered the Archbishop of Zaragoza, and the next year they tried to kill King Alfonso in Paris. They have robbed many banks, but they always give the money to the poor. Ascaso was killed in the Barcelona fighting, but Durruti has raised a militia and leads it in the hills around Zaragoza. They say he is mad, but his men and women will die for him. If it had not been for him and all the others wearing the anarchist red and black colors, the fascists might have taken the city on July 19."

"But you are not an anarchist?" asked Ted looking at the red scarf at Dolores's throat.

"I do not know," she replied. "I like them. They have fire, and they may be the only answer for the peasants. Papa says they are too undisciplined, but they are running many of the businesses and the industry in Barcelona and it is working."

"There are so many different groups," said Ted. "I don't know who they all are or who I should like and who I should be wary of."

"There are not so many," said Dolores smiling. "The largest are the anarchists, the CNT-FAI, and the socialist UGT The PSUC is socialist with a few communists. The POUM too is communist, but follow Trotsky, not Stalin. We are small, but we are well-organized. It is said we have an armored car somewhere in the city."

"Why did your father join POUM?"

"Because he prefers the structure of communism to the disorganization of the anarchists, and because he does not like the things Stalin has been doing in the Soviet Union with his purges."

"Spanish politics are very complex." Ted shook his head in wonder.

"Yes," Dolores replied with a laugh, "but we are all after the same thing. Spain is a very old country. Many people have invaded us over the centuries—the Romans, the Visigoths and the Moors—and all have left some mark. The Moors ruled southern Spain for 700 years; they gave us the Flamenco and our dark eyes. The Church and the wealthy classes want to keep us living in the past and are prepared to use force to protect their privileges. But it will not work. As soon as France and England give us some arms, you will see a Spain where all are equal and where there is no injustice."

Ted watched enthralled as Dolores, eyes flashing, described her vision of the dawning era. Her world was so different from his own, and her matter-of-fact acceptance of its violence was completely at odds with the pacifism his father had taught him back in Canada.

"People are all underneath good," Dolores continued. "They do not need police to make them that way. Capitalists tell us that, so they can use the police to keep the people…," she hesitated.

"Under control?" suggested Ted.

"Yes, that is it, under control."

Ted nodded in agreement as he thought back to his father's experience of the "On-to-Ottawa Trek" the year before. But there was still something about the idea that bothered him.

"What about the bad guys?" he asked. "If there are no police, won't there be robbers and murderers everywhere?"

"No," Dolores replied slowly as she searched for words, "laws are made by people. If many people think that murder is wrong, it will become a law. It will be written down. If you take away the writing, it will still be a law. The people will catch the bad guys and punish them."

Ted was amazed and a little overwhelmed. Dolores seemed so sure. She had an answer for everything and knew so much. Ted's opinions, which had appeared so radical and daring back home when he argued with Henry Thomas, paled beside the certainty of his new friend. Ted was eager for her to meet Will.

Their conversation and Ted's musings were rudely interrupted by another song from the driver who as they were careening around a sharp corner, took one hand completely off the wheel and began to beat out the time on the worn dashboard. Somehow they made it. Ted relaxed a little as the road straightened out for a few miles.

As they climbed onto the hot Aragon Plateau, Dolores attempted to teach Ted the rudiments of her language. This amounted to little more than a few common verbs—*ser*–to be; *comer*–to eat; *tener*–to have—and a list of useful nouns and adjectives—*agua*–water; *camino*–road; *camion*–truck; *hermana*–sister—but Ted felt that even that brought him closer to his new friend. In any case, concentrating on declining the verb "to be" took his mind off the hair-raising journey.

Friday, July 24, 1936
Afternoon

By mid-afternoon the three travelers were hot and tired. Hour after hour, they passed through progressively smaller towns, all with a distinctly chipped look and filled with tired militia. The houses were made of mud and stone and huddled almost apologetically around a central church, which was invariably being used as a storehouse and commonly had blackened walls. Scrawny chickens and desolate mules watched disinterestedly as they passed.

Eventually they came to Leciñena. The whole town had a deserted, run-down look. The only people in the streets were militia, and all the shops had been broken open and plundered. Many of the buildings were damaged in some way and quite a few were nothing more than rubble.

It was obvious there had been heavy fighting here very recently. The first thing Ted heard when the ambulance stopped was the distant rattle of gunfire. Zaragoza lay not too many miles to the west. In between, fascists and workers struggled for control of the barren land.

They had come to a stop outside the town church, which

looked just as worn and desecrated as all the others they had seen. A group of ragged, dirty men sat forlornly on its steps, many with crude bandages covering some part of their anatomy. All appeared exhausted and barely looked up as Dolores and Ted entered the building. The driver remained in his cab humming a tune to himself.

Inside Ted found a scene which made Ted wish he was back in the relative civilization of Barcelona. The smell hit him first—the sickly stink of illness and death. Ted's throat contracted and he instinctively looked at Dolores. Her face was set in a grim frown. There was little left to suggest that this had been a church only a week ago. The pews and stalls had been ripped out and the floor was covered with a thick layer of coarse straw. Lying on the straw were those wounded in the recent fighting. Many were either asleep, unconscious or dead. It was impossible to tell which. Others lay with glazed eyes staring at the vaulted ceiling far above them. A nurse moved down the rows of prostrate bodies, and with a goatskin bag expertly directed a thin stream of water into the open mouths of her patients.

At the far end of the building a doctor stood in earnest conversation with another nurse. Purposefully, Dolores strode toward him. When the doctor looked up, she launched into a long string of rapid Spanish from which Ted picked up only, "*el canadiense.*" The doctor replied at some length. He appeared agitated and waved his arms around a lot. There were dark rings under his eyes and he looked as if he hadn't slept in several nights.

At last Dolores thanked him and, motioning to Ted, retreated down the aisle.

"What did he say?" Ted asked impatiently. "Does he know where my father is?"

Dolores kept walking as she answered. "He didn't meet your father, but he thinks he was here. He said we should check at the militia headquarters in the town hall across the square." Dolores hesitated and looked at Ted.

"What is it?" he asked. "What else did he say?"

"He said we should leave. Two days ago the town was in fascist hands and the militia drove them out. Now the fascists are advancing again. He has orders to evacuate the wounded tonight as soon as enough ambulances and trucks arrive."

"I'm not leaving without my father," Ted said firmly. "I didn't come all this way just to go back on my own. My mother is depending on me to bring Dad back and reunite the family. If he's around here I'm going to find him." He stared hard at Dolores. "But maybe you should go," he said, "a girl might not be safe here."

Dolores's eyes narrowed. "Girl!" she said. "Girls are fighting and dying in the militias. Wars and revolutions are not safe. I do not want to be safe. If you want to be safe, you go back to Canada."

"Okay, okay," Ted backed off hurriedly. "It was just a

thought, I didn't mean anything. Sorry." Ted *was* sorry he had upset Dolores, but inside he was glad that she was staying. It was not just that he didn't know how he would manage without her, he really wanted to spend more time in her company.

"I'm glad you're staying. I didn't want you to go," he added quietly.

Dolores's face softened. "Okay," she said, "let us go and find Will."

The pair walked out of the church into the warm late afternoon. The driver was still behind the wheel of the ambulance. Across the cobbled square sat a large rectangular building that Ted guessed must be the town hall. Armed men were going in and out of the door and an open truck was parked to one side. A squad of about twenty soldiers lounged against the wall on the shaded side of the square. In the center stood a long stone drinking-trough with an old, wrought-iron pump at one end.

"That must be the militia building over there," said Ted, pointing across the square.

In silence they crossed to the steps leading up to the front door.

"My bag!" Ted stopped and half turned. "I've left my bag in the ambulance. I'd better go and get it."

"We can get it later," Dolores said.

Ted looked back across the square. Already, wounded

militia were being carried out of the church and into the back of the ambulance.

"No," he said, "I don't know how long we will be or when the ambulance is leaving. The bag has all my things in it. You wait here." Ted started back.

"I'll come also." Ted thought he heard Dolores sigh, then she was at his side retracing their steps. They had almost reached the water pump when they heard a low, steady drone in the sky. Dolores stopped walking and cocked her head to listen.

"What's that?" Ted asked.

"Shh," said Dolores shortly.

The drone was getting louder. The soldiers were beginning to notice. Several stood up, rifles in hand, and were scanning the sky expectantly. Then everything seemed to happen at once. Ted was watching the soldiers when one of them raised his arm and pointed. The man beside him raised his rifle. Ted looked up. He was amazed to see a plane coming straight at them—a dark, threatening shape emerging from the bright sky. All the soldiers were standing now, gesticulating and pointing their rifles. Some were firing. The plane seemed to be almost over the square. Ted felt a tug on his arm and heard Dolores's urgent shout, *"Aquí! Pronto! Pronto!"*

Then he was dragged unceremoniously down beside the drinking trough.

Ted just had time to think, "This is silly," before two deafening explosions shook the ground beneath him. He felt himself lifted into the air and thrown back down painfully. His ears felt as if they were about to explode. Ted had a vague impression of small stones hitting the cobbles all around him, then something hit him painfully in the middle of his back. As the noise of the explosions died away, Ted could hear the occasional gunshot. Somewhere nearby, someone was screaming.

Ted could feel Dolores's shoulders beneath his outstretched arm. Lifting his head he turned to look at her. His back hurt.

"Dolores, are you okay?"

Slowly she began to move.

"I think so," she replied turning a stunned gaze towards him. "Are you?"

"Yes," he said, "but my back hurts."

Sitting up, Dolores examined Ted's back.

"I'm not surprised," she commented at last, "you have been hit by a fascist bomb."

Sitting back on her heels, Dolores showed Ted a large, ugly piece of curved metal.

"I think it hit the pump and fell on you. It is lucky you were not upright. You will have some pain I think, but there is no blood."

Rolling over to sit up, Ted reached for the piece of bomb.

It was still warm to the touch. Looking up, the pair were faced with a scene of devastation. Ted gasped. The town hall was a ruin. All its windows were blown out and a column of smoke was rising from a large hole in the roof. The front door hung forlornly at a crazy angle. Dazed figures were standing or sitting on the steps.

Ted and Dolores stared silently for a moment, unable to believe their luck. Ted turned to survey the rest of the square. Behind them the squad of militia were still against the wall. Most appeared to be unhurt, although two or three lay on the cobbles with comrades hunched over them. Turning to look at the church, Ted saw where the second bomb had fallen. The building itself appeared undamaged, but there was a large, blackened hole in the ground emitting clouds of dark smoke. The surface of the square around the hole was covered with fragments of cobblestone. Bodies were scattered about like abandoned toys. The nurses and the doctor from the hospital were already attending to the wounded. The ambulance lay nearby, a tangled mass of metal. It was upside down and the cab was crushed level with the hood. One wheel turned lazily in the sunlight. There was no sign of the German driver.

Ted felt weak. How lucky could you get? If they had been in the militia headquarters, or back at the ambulance, they would probably be dead. He sat down heavily on the edge of the water trough.

"What are we going to do now?" he asked, as much to himself as Dolores. It was obvious that they could get no help from the militia headquarters.

"I think, that we must seek your father on our own," she answered without moving her eyes from the smoking building.

"But your father said not to leave the aid station."

"They cannot help us," she said looking at Ted. "No one here can help us. My father was mistaken to think we would be safe here. The plane might, even now, be returning with a fresh load of bombs. At least we will be safer in the countryside."

"I suppose you're right." Ted's voice sounded calm, but he couldn't stop his hands from shaking.

Friday, July 24, 1936
Evening

❧━━━━━━━━━━━❧

The sun was low in the sky when the pair left Leciñena. There were only a few hours of daylight left, but the two had decided to start just in case the plane returned with more bombs. They filled a couple of water bottles at the pump, and helped themselves to some stale bread and cheese from a shop that had had its front blown completely open. No one was around, but Dolores left a few coins on the dust-covered counter in case someone returned. Ted had wanted to leave something too, but the tiny amount of money he had was in French centimes, and would be of little use to an Aragonese peasant.

Munching on the dry bread, they walked west towards the sound of the guns. Isolated soldiers, some wounded, passed them in the opposite direction. Occasional trucks forced them off the road. At every opportunity, Dolores asked a passersby if they knew of a Canadian who had arrived a couple of days ago. The only replies she received were shaken heads.

By dusk, they were both tired. The truck traffic heading

for Lecineña had increased noticeably and they were beginning to see groups of militiamen who were not obviously wounded. Most passed with lowered eyes, giving no response to Dolores's inquiries, but a few looked up and gesticulated back the way they had come. *"Los fascistas,"* they mumbled before returning to their trudge down the road.

"We must find somewhere for the night." Dolores was looking at a cluster of buildings through a grove of stunted olive trees. "In the dark we could easily become mislaid."

"Lost," Ted corrected automatically. He certainly didn't want to become mislaid. What he really wanted was to stop walking on the sharp stones of the road in his unsuitable shoes. "Maybe they will let us sleep in the barn."

"I think there is no one there," said Dolores, heading down the embankment and through the trees, "It is a hacienda of a landowner."

As usual, Dolores was right. There was a small complex of buildings, all completely empty. What had once been the main house was nothing more than a blackened ruin, standing in the twilight as a stark reminder of the peasants' hatred for the landlords. A large barn had a gaping hole where its doors had been, but otherwise appeared in good shape. There was no sign of any livestock.

"I guess no one will mind if we sleep in the barn," said Ted, heading towards the building.

It took time for their eyes to become accustomed to the

gloomy interior, but they soon made out the shapes of assorted farm machinery, piles of hay bales and rows of animal stalls. The last stall was filled with fresh straw.

"This looks like the best place," said Ted, slumping down exhausted against one of the walls. The smell of the recent animal occupants was strong, but Ted didn't mind as long as he didn't have to stand on his aching feet any longer. Dolores sat down beside him and produced some cheese from her shoulder bag. They ate in silence as the fading light of the sun was replaced by the light of a full moon. As they finished eating, the interior of the barn became bathed in an eerie silver glow, which highlighted the sharp contours of the machinery and cast odd shadows on the walls.

"Do you think we will find Will?" asked Ted eventually.

"Yes," Dolores replied. "He must have come this way, and it will not be easy for a tall Canadian to hide in a Spanish militia. Tomorrow we will find the militia commander. He will know and then you will be united."

"Yes," said Ted, "probably," and in his thoughts he continued, "and then we will go back to Barcelona and then to Perpignan and my mother, and I will never see you again." Ted found it hard to believe it had been only two days since he had left his mother and only one day since he had met Dolores. So much had happened: he had been shot at; almost killed by a mad ambulance driver; and bombed. This was cer-

tainly not like his life in the Okanagan Valley. He didn't
know how he would have managed without Dolores.

Ted looked over at his companion. She was sitting beside
him, the moonlight illuminating her profile. She was so different from anyone he had ever met—confident and knowl-
edgeable, and concerned about what was going on. No one
back in Canada, except Will, seemed to care half as much as
she did. Certainly not sniveling little bourgeois fascists like
Henry Thomas and his father. Ted smiled at his language.

Revolutionary jargon. He had heard plenty of it at the
meetings he had been to with Will, and it always sounded
affected to him. People often seemed to say it just because it
was the right thing to say at meetings. Yet here, in the midst
of revolution and war, the words seemed to mean something
more. Ted was amazed at the sense of camaraderie he felt.
Everyone really did appear to be equal. Dolores was so lucky
to be living through this. And she was so beautiful.

As if in response to his unspoken thought, Dolores
turned to look at Ted. The moonlight lit her cheeks and
forehead, but her eyes were black, like two deep wells.

"What are you thinking?" she asked.

Ted suddenly felt awkward and embarrassed. His cheeks
flushed, and he was glad of the pale light.

"Oh, nothing," he said haltingly.

As if she knew he was lying, Dolores smiled. Ted felt
weak, as if he had no will of his own, no strength, no exis-

tence apart from the face in front of him. That smile was a killer. And her eyes. Ted had loved them from the first moment he had seen them coming toward Rafael Martinez's desk, but now he was staring into them. He felt like he was falling. Falling into those eyes which were so deep they had no bottom. He didn't think he would ever be able to find his way out. He didn't care. He didn't want a way out.

Their faces were only inches apart. Their noses bumped awkwardly. Dolores smiled again and tilted her head. Their lips met. Then the straw around them erupted. Dolores screamed. Straw filled Ted's eyes and nose. In frantic confusion, he wiped it away and looked over at Dolores, but she wasn't looking at him. Dolores was staring across the stall at a man holding a revolver. Propped up on one elbow and covered with straw, he looked more like a discarded scarecrow than a man, but there was no mistaking the intention behind the gun. It was pointed unwaveringly at Ted's head.

No one spoke. Ted examined the man. He did not look well. He was dressed in an unfamiliar dark blue uniform which was covered in dried mud. A red beret was perched over a face that was strained and thin and that sported several days growth of beard. His appearance was frightening, but his eyes were uncertain; they flickered indecisively from one of his prisoners to the other. For a brief moment, Ted hoped that the red beret signified that the man was a communist or socialist.

"Who…?" Ted began.

"Fascist," Dolores almost spat the word out. The gun swung over to cover her.

"But we're behind government lines." Ted couldn't believe a fascist had been hiding in the straw all this time.

"The fascists were here only two days ago," Dolores explained. "The doctor said so. This one must have been left behind."

"Silencio!" The man's voice was not strong, but Ted and Dolores both obeyed his command instantly. They watched as the man maneuvered himself into a sitting position. The gun wavered, but remained pointed at them. The man was in obvious pain and used his free hand to haul his legs in front of him. Ted noticed his trousers were torn in many places and soaked in blood. That was why he was here. The soldier had been wounded in the fascist retreat and left behind. He must have been hiding in the straw for at least two days.

Gesticulating with the gun and using curt orders which Dolores translated, the man forced Ted and Dolores to stand and empty their pockets. When he was satisfied that they were not armed, he ordered them to sit against the wall across the stall from him.

"Agua," he said, pointing at Dolores's water bottle lying in the straw. When she passed it over, he uncorked it and drank greedily until it was empty. Then he pointed to what was left of the bread and cheese, and ate as if he had never

seen food before. Ted's water bottle was also emptied.

While he ate, the man never took his eyes off his prisoners. Ted's mind filled with images of himself diving forward to knock the gun aside, wrestling it from the man and escaping into the night with Dolores. The man didn't look strong and Ted was convinced he could overpower him, but the distance between them was too great. The gun would come round and Ted would be dead before he made it halfway across the stall. There was no chance for heroics here. Ted wondered what his father would do in the same circumstances. Would he resort to violence?

The three figures sat in the moonlight looking at one another. Every time Ted and Dolores tried to talk, the man said, *"Silencio,"* and waggled his gun. Dolores tried talking to the soldier. She told him her name and Ted's, and asked his. There was no response. Dolores spoke slowly and Ted understood the occasional word. She seemed to be talking about the revolution, and Ted assumed she was trying to persuade him over to their side. But there was no response and, eventually, Dolores fell silent.

The man sat still, watching them. His face was gray in the moonlight. Occasionally, it twist in pain, but the gun never wavered. The man's hand rested on his thigh and the gun barrel pointed straight across at the pair. When Dolores spoke, the gun swung over to point at her. When she stopped, it swung back to Ted. Ted wasn't keen on the way

Spaniards kept pointing guns at him.

Ted began to contemplate the future. Obviously, the soldier wasn't going to shoot them out of hand, otherwise, he would have done so already. Equally obviously, he wasn't going anywhere with his legs the way they were. So they seemed destined to stay in the stall until something happened. Ted thought the most likely thing to happen was that someone from the militia would show up. Basically that would be good news, although Ted didn't relish the thought of being caught in the barn if the soldier panicked. Ted's plan of action was to stay awake and hope that either the soldier fell asleep or the militia showed up and distracted their captor enough to give Ted a chance to grab the gun. It wasn't much of a plan, Ted admitted to himself, but he could come up with no other. The three sat contemplating one another.

After what must have been hours, Ted felt Dolores slump against him: she was asleep at last. Her head rested on his shoulder and Ted felt her soft hair against his cheek. Gently, he rested his head against hers. It was good she was getting some rest—he would stay awake and await his chance. Ted stared across at the soldier, willing him to nod off, but the pale, immobile face stared straight back at him. The night was warm, the straw was comfortable and the man was wounded; surely he would go to sleep soon. But it was Ted who fell asleep first. He couldn't stop himself. His vision blurred and his head kept nodding forward only to be jerked back as he struggled to stay awake. Gradually, Ted slipped into a disturbed sleep filled with dreams of barns he had played in as a boy and orchards he had snuck into to steal apples, cherries and plums. They were good dreams, just like the carefree summer days of his childhood, except that Dolores was in them. She was running with him through the orchards, but no matter how hard Ted tried to catch her, she always stayed tantalizingly out of reach. Ted's sleeping face alternated between smiles and frowns. Across from him, the soldier maintained his stony vigil.

Saturday, July 25, 1936
First Light

❧————————————❧

When Ted awoke, pale sunlight was filtering through the cracks in the barn walls. At first he couldn't remember where he was. The animal smell, the feel of the straw and his half-remembered dreams took him back home. Ted was still smiling as he opened his eyes, but the smile faded the moment he saw the soldier sitting across from him.

The man was inhuman; he was still awake. The eyes stared coldly at Ted. At some time in the night, Dolores had slipped off his shoulder and now lay curled in the hay beside him. Ted's gaze slid over to the gun which still pointed straight at his stomach. Morbidly, he began to wonder what it was like to be shot in the stomach. Somewhere he had read that it was the worst place to be shot and led to a lingering, painful death. A spot immediately below his navel began to itch uncontrollably. Slowly, Ted moved his hand over and scratched. The gun stayed still. Now he needed to stretch. He ached all over after hours of sleeping in a sitting position. Slowly, he raised his arms and flexed his muscles. The gun remained stationary. Ted returned his gaze to the soldier's face. The eyes hadn't moved. Ted tried to outstare the soldier. He lost. His eyes began to sting and tear and he was forced to blink. The soldier stared on impassively. Ted frowned. Painfully slowly, he moved to the right. The soldier's stare remained where Ted's head had been. The eyes didn't follow him. Something was wrong. Cautiously, Ted drew his legs up underneath himself and rocked forward. Dolores groaned in her sleep. The soldier didn't move.

Ted's lunge was less acrobatic and stylish than the one he had imagined the night before, but it was fast and powerful. Focusing on the gun, Ted closed his fingers over the cold metal. There was no deafening crash, no tearing pain, no bullet. Just a cold feeling and the sense that the soldier was falling over. Ted didn't want to pull the gun in case it went off, but he expected the soldier to struggle and start hitting him. His hope was that he could remain in control of the gun until Dolores found something with which to hit the soldier. But there was no struggle. Instead Ted could hear Dolores asking groggily, *"Qué pasa?"*

Ted felt the soldier's legs, stiff and unmoving beneath him. The hand holding the gun was as cold as the gunmetal itself. Still holding onto the gun, Ted rolled off the man, and looked up. The force of Ted's attack had knocked the soldier onto his side. He lay like a china doll, his dark eyes staring straight at the wall. His left arm, which Ted had assumed was resting on the pile of straw beside him, now pointed awkwardly up in the air. The straw underneath and all around Ted was a congealing mass of blood. The soldier had been dead for many hours.

Ted grimaced and moved away from the body. The gun pointed uselessly into the straw. Ted turned to see Dolores looking at the corpse with a stunned expression on her face.

"He's dead," said Ted unnecessarily. "Rigor mortis has set in, so he has been dead for a while. I guess the activity last night opened his wounds and he bled to death."

The pair stared at the dead soldier. Outside, it was getting brighter, which only made the whole scene somehow less real. A sharp line of shadow was slowly moving across the stall wall. It had almost reached the grotesquely up-stretched arm of the body. Eventually Ted spoke.

"I suppose we should get his gun," he said tentatively, hoping that Dolores would say no.

Dolores, who was being uncharacteristically quiet, nodded. She seemed mesmerized by the body.

Careful not to step in the mass of bloodstained straw, Ted moved over to the soldier. The man's hand was locked around the gun's grip, but his finger was outside the trigger guard. If Ted needed to pull hard, he was unlikely to be shot by a dead man. Reaching down he gave a tentative pull. The body moved. Ted shivered and pulled harder. Someone tapped him on the back. Gasping, Ted let go of the gun and jumped back. Then he laughed nervously. When Ted had pulled on the gun, the soldier's outstretched arm had been pulled over, bumping Ted's back.

Ted took a deep breath and returned to his gruesome task. The soldier's arm felt welded to the thigh on which it had rested all night. There was no way Ted would get the gun simply by pulling it. He tried to pry the soldier's fingers loose one by one. No good. The hand was like cold marble. Ted shuddered and stood up.

"It's no use," he said turning to Dolores, "I can't move his hand." In a way Ted felt relieved. Getting the gun seemed the obvious thing to do, but Ted knew his father would not have approved. He could almost hear Will saying, "What's the point of having a gun if you are not prepared to use it? And using a gun is never justified. It only leads to pain and suffering." Ted was just as happy without the weapon.

"Come on," Ted stepped back and took Dolores by the hand. "Let's get out of here."

Outside, the sun was already above the horizon. Ted could feel its warmth on his face. The sky was clear and he immediately felt cleaner. In the sunlight, Dolores shrugged off her preoccupation with the soldier and looked around.

"Well," said Ted, nodding back at the barn, "I think he ate our breakfast last night."

"Yes," Dolores agreed. "Ted," she continued, turning towards him, "I was very much scared in there. Thank you."

Not knowing what to say, Ted smiled. Dolores stepped

forward, put her arms around his neck and kissed him on the cheek. Then she gave him a long hug.

"Come on," she said, brushing the straw off her clothes. "I think we should go back to the road."

Hand in hand, the pair set off through the olive trees.

Unlike the night before, the road was deserted. It ran in a straight line for a considerable distance before curving behind some rugged rock outcrops. On either side, olive groves spread out in the distance. Ted was happy at the prospect of walking with Dolores. The terrifying images of the night before were melting in the morning sun.

They had been walking for about ten minutes when the figures appeared ahead of them. It was a squad of soldiers marching in loose order with a solitary figure, who Ted assumed was their officer, striding at the front.

"At last," Ted remarked, "someone to ask about Will."

As they neared the figures, Ted sensed Dolores hesitate.

"What's the matter?" he asked.

Although the figures were still a considerable distance away, Dolores's voice was barely above a whisper.

"Fascists," she replied nervously. "Look at their hats."

Sure enough, the approaching men were all wearing the same red berets as the soldier in the barn. Ted felt a cold ring tightening around his heart. They were trapped. They couldn't turn around, the soldiers would easily catch them or shoot them. The olive trees bordering the road were too far apart to provide cover if they tried to run to either side. They would be hunted down without difficulty. All they could do was walk straight ahead and pray that they could bluff it out.

"Keep walking and smile a lot," Ted whispered as he glanced over at his companion. Thank heavens she wasn't wearing the blue overalls that seemed to be the closest thing the militia had to a uniform. Then his heart sank.

"Your red scarf," he breathed urgently. Dolores's jaw muscles tense at his words. Slowly her hand came up and undid the knot at her throat. Crumpling the damning piece of cloth in her palm, she lowered her hand and stuffed it into her pocket. The scarf would probably have been a death sentence. Ted was relieved that he had not been able to get the gun. It would have been too big to hide, and its presence, too suspicious.

The squad was close now, and Ted could feel the officer looking at them. Dolores's hand was clenching his like an iron vice. Ted forced himself to smile. As they drew level with the soldiers, he nodded and forced his smile wider. The officer's eyes bored into him.

"If he talks to us, we're doomed," Ted thought. The sound of the soldier's boots was almost drowned out by the pounding of his heart. Every soldier seemed to be turning his head to look straight at him.

"They must know who we are," he said to himself. This

was taking forever. Ted could feel the sweat forming under his arms and pouring down his sides. He didn't know how he kept going. They were almost at the end of the column. Maybe they would make it. Through the haze of his fear, Ted was vaguely aware that the sound of the soldier's marching boots had ceased. Then came the voice, urgent and allowing no denial.

"*Alto!*"

Ted and Dolores froze in mid-step. Ted could hear footsteps approaching. Slowly he turned. The officer was striding towards them. He was looking at Dolores. Ted was dismayed to see that he had drawn his pistol, though he held it down by his side. When he reached the pair, the officer gazed for a long moment at each of them. Then his eyes moved down Dolores. Ted followed the man's gaze as it halted at the incriminating splash of red hanging from her pocket. Abruptly the officer reached over with his free hand and pulled the scarf free. Triumphantly he held it up in front of them.

"*Socialista? Anarchista?*" he sneered. Ted could think of nothing to say. The smile had long ago faded from his lips. In one movement, the officer dropped the scarf, grabbed Dolores's collar and jerked her head back. He raised his pistol and pressed it into her temple. There was a deafening click as his thumb pulled back the hammer.

"Noooo!" Ted screamed. "Canadian! Canadian!

Canadian!"

The officer hesitated. He turned to look at Ted, but the muzzle of the gun remained firmly against Dolores's head. Ted's mind raced. Time slowed almost to a stop. What had Dolores taught him in the ambulance a lifetime ago?

"*Nosotros somos canadiense,*" he stammered. "*Ella es mi…,*" sister, what was the word for sister? Dolores had said it. Ted's mind raced back over their conversation in the ambulance. Fear made his memory incredibly vivid. He could see himself sitting in the dusty cab, listening to the German driver singing in the background. Dolores was teaching him the names of family members, "*Padre, Madre, Hermano…*"

"*Hermana,*" he almost shouted. "*Ella es mi hermana. Nosotros somos…*on holiday, vacation." He didn't know the word.

"*Vacación,*" Dolores's voice was husky, but her eyes were strangely calm. She deliberately pronounced the word haltingly. The officer turned his gaze back to Dolores. Slowly he released her collar and lowered his pistol. Ted sighed. Time returned to something like its normal speed. The officer held out his hand.

"*Pasaporte,*" he said.

Ted pulled his battered passport out of his pocket. The officer thumbed rapidly through it. In a moment he would ask for Dolores's papers and then they would be sunk. Ted talked rapidly.

"We are on holiday—Canadians on a hiking holiday. We didn't hear what had happened until we got caught up in the fighting. We're just trying to find our way north to get home. Back to Canada. We're not a part of this war. We want to find the nearest Canadian consul—*consular*. Can you help us? Where would that be? *Dondé está el consular canadiense?*"

Ted was babbling and he knew it. He was even making up words that sounded Spanish. But he doubted if it mattered. The officer probably didn't understand anything he was saying except maybe the word Canada, so Ted kept repeating that as often as he could. The officer hesitated. At that moment, a burst of heavy firing sounded in the distance from the direction of Leciñena. The officer looked up. Closing Ted's passport, he holstered his pistol, turned and barked out a series of commands to his soldiers. Two men put down their rifles and stepped hurriedly forward. One stood behind Dolores, the other behind Ted. Strong hands gripped his arms above the elbows, pinning them to his side. The officer stepped forward, roughly tore Ted's shirt open and pulled it away from his shoulders. Apparently satisfied, he repeated the action with Dolores.

More orders, and a soldier with stripes on his arms, probably a sergeant, stepped forward. The officer handed him Ted's passport and, gesticulating down the road, gave him some orders. As the main body of troops resumed their interrupted march, the sergeant led Ted and Dolores in the direction they had originally been heading. The two other soldiers, each with an evil-looking bayonet attached to his rifle, followed along behind. Ted's heart rate was almost back to normal. He looked over at Dolores.

"We were lucky," he said with understatement.

"Yes we were," Dolores agreed. "Very. They were about to shoot us. That was quick thinking. Thank you again."

Ted almost felt like smiling.

"It was all I could think of," he said. "Thank you for teaching me a few words. But why did they look at our shoulders?"

"To see if we had fired a rifle recently. If they had found bruises, they would have shot us, Canadian or not."

"*Silencio,*" the man in front spat over his shoulder.

Both obeyed instantly. In silence they trudged down the road to the unknown with only their thoughts for company.

Saturday, July 25, 1936
Morning

⟡————————⟡

After about an hour, the group came to a hacienda which was being used as the local headquarters. The main house had a ramshackle look, but was still intact. Its courtyard was filled with soldiers and several officers were organizing them into marching columns. No one paid the newcomers any attention as they marched up the steps of the building. Inside was equally busy, although there were far more officers about. Everyone seemed to be going some-where with a worried look on his face. There were several striking differences between these men and the government forces: all these soldiers wore the same uniform; each seemed to be armed with a fairly new rifle; there were no women sol-diers here; and there was a much stronger sense of authority. Men stood at attention when talking to an officer and every-one saluted as they passed. This was a real army. It certainly appeared much more efficient than the comradely collection of armed workers Ted had seen before.

Encouraged by the bayonets of their guards, Ted and Dolores were herded into a spacious, elegant room which had once been the drawing room. Pictures of horses and men in uniform hung on the walls and a grand piano stood to one side. The piano's top was covered with open maps and several officers stood around studying them. Ted watched nervously as the sergeant crossed the room and made his report. When he handed over Ted's passport, everyone looked across at the pair. Ted felt very conspicuous under their gaze. Eventually, one of the officers gave an order and the group returned to their planning.

With a few curt commands to the guards, the sergeant led Ted and Dolores across the crowded courtyard. He stopped when he reached the barn, apparently uncertain where to go next. There were several smaller buildings scattered around the barn like chicks round a mother hen. After some thought, the sergeant motioned his small group to the right. The barn was set at an angle to the courtyard and they had to cross in front of its open doors to reach their destination. As they passed, Ted glanced into the dark interior. He could not see much, only the shape of a large open car with three figures standing by the driver's door. It struck Ted as odd that, in the middle of all this military activity, these people should be dressed in civilian clothes, but he didn't really have time to think about it.

One of the figures wore a long, dark, leather coat and held a map case in front of him. As Ted passed, the man looked up and gestured to a soldier who pushed the door closed. It was all over in a moment, but the scene bothered Ted. The man in the coat looked out of place. He was tall, blond and had strong chiseled features that didn't look Spanish. Even more disturbing was that one of the other men in the shadows seemed strangely familiar.

As Ted and Dolores turned the corner, they saw a low stone wall forming a small enclosure against the side of the barn. It looked and smelled like a pigsty. Several soldiers lounged against the wall smoking. Each had a rifle propped beside him and each looked up as the small party came into view. The sergeant stopped and Ted had a chance to take in more details. What he saw horrified him.

The barn wall was chipped and covered with dark splashes. The same dark liquid formed puddles at the base of the wall where the mud was heavily churned up. A trail, as if weights had been dragged over the mud, led from the barn to a gate in the low wall.

One of the soldiers spoke to the sergeant, whose reply triggered laughter amongst the men. The sergeant spoke again. The man answered, pointing to the back of the barn. The sergeant turned and herded his captives back the way they had come. He led Ted and Dolores to a small stone building. A soldier with a rifle stood outside. After a brief conversation with the sergeant, he unlocked the door and Ted and Dolores were shoved roughly into the gloomy interior.

The inside of the building measured about ten by ten with

a flagstone floor and a high roof. Three narrow, high-set windows provided some light but, despite the sunlight outside, the air inside was cold. Sprawled around the walls were about a dozen militiamen. None appeared wounded, but they all looked dirty, ragged and tired. They glanced up apathetically at the two new arrivals. Ted found a small patch of floor, and led Dolores over to sit down. The stone was cold beneath them.

The pair sat in silence for a long time. Ted could not forget the chipped, stained wall. At last he turned to Dolores and asked, "What did the soldier say?"

Several heads turned at the sound of a foreign voice. Dolores replied slowly, "He asked our guard if he had brought some new customers," she said. "Then our guard replied, 'No, not yet, these ones are being kept for after the siesta.'"

The pair sat absorbing the significance of what they had heard and witnessed. Eventually, Ted spoke.

"They won't shoot us," he said as convincingly as he could. "If they had been going to shoot us they would have done it by the road."

Dolores looked up meeting Ted's gaze. "They will shoot us," she said simply. "I think the officer on the road did not want the responsibility of shooting a foreigner. I think here they will not be so cautious," she smiled ruefully, "and sooner or later, they will realize I am a Spaniard."

Dolores was right. Sooner or later, someone would think

of looking for her passport and that would be the end of their brother/sister charade. They would also notice that Ted had crossed the border well after the revolt began and could not be the innocent hiker he claimed.

The situation looked grim. Ted didn't want to die, just when he was beginning to experience a life worth living. And what about his parents? His family was scattered now, his father missing and his mother ill in a hospital bed far from home. No one had the least idea where anyone else was. Even if his mother woke up and his parents eventually found each other again, they would not have the faintest idea what had become of their son. Despite his fear, Ted still felt a glimmer of hope. Just maybe, these soldiers might also not want to shoot a Canadian. Just maybe he would be taken to a large town like Zaragoza and sent home. But there was no hope for Dolores. No protection. Rafael Martinez would never know what had happened to his beautiful daughter.

Ted shivered. Unbidden, his mind slipped back to the image of the dead soldier of the night before. They had left him less than two hours ago, yet it seemed like a lifetime. The front lines must have passed them while they sat in the barn. The wounded man had almost made it. Ted wondered if he might have survived the night if it had not been for the activity he had been forced into by Ted and Dolores's arrival. There was no point in worrying about that now; their horrific imprisonment was a much more immediate concern.

Ted looked around to see if there was any means of escape. There was not. The room was well chosen as a prison. Its walls were solid and there was only one, heavy door. The floor was stone and the windows were too small to allow anyone to climb through, even if they had not been positioned so far out of reach. In the gloom, the prisoners looked like discarded sacks of grain. Each was slumped against the wall, head on chest, dwelling on a terribly uncertain future. The silence was becoming unbearably oppressive. Everyone sat, without hope, waiting for the worst to happen.

Ted desperately wanted to say something positive, something hopeful, something of the world outside this prison.

"Have you ever been to a bullfight?" he asked abruptly. It sounded silly, but it was the only topic he could think of that might take their minds off what was happening.

Dolores looked surprised. "What?" she asked.

"A bullfight. Do you like bullfights?"

"No," replied Dolores indignantly, "fighting bulls are raised by rich landowners in Andalucia. For a bull to be brave in the ring, it must never see a man on foot while being raised. This requires much land which could be used by the peasants for farming. It is just another way that the poor are exploited."

Ted was silent. He hadn't thought about that when he had read Hemingway's descriptions of huge bull ranches run by families who had been breeding famous fighting bulls for generations. He had only seen the production of a fearless machine, created for one purpose only—to provide a worthy opponent for the frail man who must face it in the ring. Another assumption was proving more complicated then he had previously suspected.

"But yes," Dolores continued in a wistful voice, "despite that, I do like the bullfight. My father is an aficionado. As a boy he saw Joselito and Belmonte, and he used to take me to the fights on Easter Sunday at the Plaza Monumental before my mother was killed. That was where I saw your American torero, Sidney Franklin.

"I loved the bullfight as a child—the suits of lights, the beauty of the bulls, the pageantry, the bravery of the matador. My father told me that the very first time he took me when I was just a little child, he was afraid I would cry when the horses were killed. I didn't, I laughed. The poor things looked so awkward and funny, staggering around after the bull had gored them. I did not know what death was. But I did cry when the bull was killed. I had wanted him to win and I was sad when he fell over."

Ted could just make out Dolores's face in the gloom.

"Have you ever seen a bullfight?" she asked.

"No," Ted admitted, "I was hoping to see one on this trip. My mother didn't think it was a good idea. She said it was cruel."

"Yes," agreed Dolores, "to some people it is cruel. Many visitors to Spain think it is a barbaric pastime. But I think they do not take the time to understand. Spain has a very violent past—a long history of death. Romans, Moors and French killed us and we killed them. And, we have killed each other. The Church tortured and killed us in the name of Christ. The anarchists killed the priests and nuns in the name of freedom. There is a fascist general who leads his legionnaires into battle, screaming 'Long Live Death.' I think maybe the death of a bull does not mean the same to us."

"I would still like to see one."

"You should. You will understand us better. Unfortunately, there are not many now, although it is the height of the season. It seems most of the matadors are supporters of the fascists."

Dolores fell silent. Ted was struggling to think of a new topic which wouldn't end in a discussion of death, when the door opened. A shaft of harsh sunlight cut through the room. Squinting against the glare, Ted could just make out a figure with a rifle. He felt his heart beat faster. The figure was saying something, but was having difficulty. The words sounded like, "Aydooard reean."

The voice was guttural and exhibited increasing signs of frustration as each pronouncement was met with stony silence. Ted wanted desperately to ask Dolores what the man was saying, but he didn't want to draw attention to himself. He glanced at his companion. She was staring at him with a very odd expression on her face. It was partly sadness, partly fear, and partly confusion. Ted frowned. Then his blood turned cold and he knew; "Aydooard reean" was a Spanish attempt to say Edward Ryan. The man with the rifle was calling his name.

The saliva in Ted's mouth disappeared. He swallowed uncomfortably. He had to stand up and go to the door before the man became even angrier. But he wasn't sure his legs would hold him. Ted leaned forward into a crouch. Every pair of eyes in the room was watching him, but Ted refused to move his gaze from Dolores. As he stood, she reached forward and grasped his hand. For a single moment, they were physically connected. *"Viene aquí!"* came the voice from the doorway. There was no mistaking the order. Ted stumbled to the door, blinking in the light. The soldier prodded him painfully in the ribs with his rifle. But Ted hardly noticed, he was being prodded towards the main house and away from the pigsty.

Saturday, July 25, 1936
Afternoon

Ted entered the hacienda for the second time that day. This time the soldier led him past the drawing room and up a wide staircase. At the top, the soldier strode over to a closed door and knocked loudly. He was answered by a voice from inside. Opening the door, the soldier roughly pushed Ted through before retreating down the stairs.

The room was smaller than the one downstairs and had obviously been ransacked. Faded squares and rectangles on the walls showed where pictures had been, and broken pieces of furniture were piled hastily into a corner. Only a couch and armchair, both covered with dusty, white sheets, remained. A large window overlooked the courtyard. The one person in the room stood by the fireplace with his back to the door. He turned, as Ted looked over. The man was dressed in a light, loosely-fitting suit. His shirt was immaculately pressed. Ted gasped and almost collapsed. He knew this man, but, Uncle Roger had been dead for almost a year, burned beyond recognition in a plane crash. How could he be here, standing by a fireplace in Spain, calmly regarding his horror-struck nephew?

"You're dead," was all Ted could manage.

Uncle Roger smiled weakly. "Apparently not," he said. "So it *is* you Ted. I wondered when I caught that glimpse of you from the barn. What on earth are you doing here?"

Ted ignored the question. He had too many of his own.

"The plane crash in the desert. You and the pilot were killed. We inherited your money."

"Not my money," the smile stayed around Roger's mouth, "some of the British government's money. These are complicated times, Ted. Things are not always as they seem. How did you get here?"

"I'm here looking for my dad. We came to Europe with your…with the inheritance, and he came down here to see what was happening."

"So Will's politics are still getting him into trouble," Roger interrupted. Then his face became more serious. "Where's Sis? Is she here too?"

"No," replied Ted, "Mom is back in Perpignan. She's sick. After Will left, we got caught in a riot and she was hit on the head. She's in a hospital, but she won't wake up. I was scared, I didn't know if Will would ever find us again, so I came to find him and take him back. Then I got caught up in all this mess."

Roger looked worried. "When did you leave her?" he asked.

"Three days ago." Ted wondered, was that all it was?

"And how long before that was she hit on the head?"

"Another two days," Ted replied.

"But you don't know what has happened to her since you left?"

"No." Ted was beginning to feel like he was being interrogated.

Ted suddenly felt very tired. What was happening? Everything he had been through these last few days was so bizarre. He didn't know why Roger was alive, though it was a relief to be able to talk to a familiar figure. Roger looked at him thoughtfully.

"So you came down on the Republican side, came out here looking for Will and got caught up in the advance?"

Ted nodded.

"You are a very lucky person to be alive."

Ted nodded again. He knew that all right. Then another thought struck him.

"Are you fighting for the fascists?" he asked.

"No," replied Roger, "I'm not fighting for anyone—yet. But I suppose you deserve some kind of explanation."

Roger crossed the room and pulled the sheets off the surviving furniture, exposing obviously expensive, floral upholstery.

"We might as well be comfortable," he said, indicating the armchair to Ted and settling himself on the couch. Ted perched on the edge of the comfortable seat. He didn't want to be too comfortable. It would be easier to keep his guard up and, anyway, he felt guilty lounging on a chair while Dolores sat worrying on the cold floor of the prison.

"For the last three years," Roger began, "I have been working for the British government. That's who I have been traveling for. When I last visited you I was on my way to Japan and China to see what was happening there. I posed as a businessman selling British steel for tanks and guns. I find that ammunition sales opens a lot of doors.

"I'm not the wealthy wastrel Will thinks I am. Strange things are happening all over the world and it is my job to find out what I can about these things. Many people feel there is going to be another war—Hitler, Mussolini and maybe even Japan, against the democracies. The more we can know about their preparedness, the better we can prepare."

"You're a spy," Ted interrupted. Roger smiled.

"I suppose you could call me that, though I don't lurk in dark alleys or leave coded messages in hollow trees. These days, the really important decisions are made in company boardrooms, not on the map tables of five-star generals. So I sit in boardrooms and listen. Then I report back.

"Your father and I are alike in many ways; we both think Hitler is evil and that war is coming. But I don't share his pacifism. There are times when you have to fight to preserve something worthwhile or to prevent a great evil from spreading. Your father and I also disagree about the reasons why this war will be fought. Will thinks Hitler wants to destroy his precious socialism, but he's wrong. Its true, Hitler will destroy any socialist he can lay his hands on. And he will persecute the Jews. In time, he will even invade his neighbors to create a 'Greater Germany,' but that is just to establish his power base. As soon as Hitler feels secure enough, he will attack Romania and Russia."

"Because Russia is communist," Ted interrupted again.

"No," Roger replied, "to get oil. Germany has no oil and needs it desperately to fuel industry, to build armies—to be strong. It is unthinkable to Hitler that Germany must rely so heavily on Britain or America for such a vital resource, so, eventually he will move to secure his own oil supply. The closest oil fields to Germany are in Romania and the Russian Caucasus. Japan faces the same problem. Ultimately, she will invade Malaya and Burma to try and take those oil fields from the British. If we can track the development of heavy industry in these countries, we will know how much they rely on oil, and be able to guess when they will go to war."

"Will thinks the revolution in Spain will lead to war." What Roger was saying seemed to make sense, but Ted couldn't sit back and let everything his father had told him be denied.

"I'm afraid your dad is wrong." Roger seemed very

relaxed and confident, sitting back on the couch. "There will be foreign involvement in Spain. Already the rebels are negotiating with Hitler and Mussolini for planes, tanks and soldiers."

"But Canada won't let them do that," Ted exclaimed.

Roger's smile broadened.

"Canada can do nothing without Britain," he replied, "and Britain will sit back and watch. In any case, your Prime Minister King greatly admires Hitler. King thinks Hitler has nice eyes. No, there will be no help for the Spanish government. Russia may make some noises, but will not do much. A few idealists will come and die for what they believe but the rebels will eventually win. Europe is not yet ready for another big war."

Ted sat silently thinking of Dolores and all the wild, brave, disorganized men and women he had seen. If what Roger said was true, they were doomed. A loud knock on the door interrupted his thoughts. Roger stood up and said something in Spanish. The door opened and the tall, blond man in the leather coat entered. He looked coldly at Ted. Roger stepped forward and the pair began an animated conversation, to Ted's surprise, in German. The talk was quite heated and Ted was dismayed to see the stranger point at him a number of times. Finally they were finished. With one last look in Ted's direction, the tall man turned and strode angrily out the door. Roger returned to the couch. He wasn't smiling any more.

"You were speaking German," Ted said slowly. "Is that man German? Are you working for the Germans?"

Roger regarded Ted thoughtfully for a moment before replying.

"This is all rather unfortunate. Yes, Helmut is German, he works for the Luftwaffe—the German air force. He is here to examine what role they might play in Spain." Roger glanced at the closed door and dropped his voice. "As to your second question, no, I do not work for the Germans, but it is convenient for the moment that they think I do. That is why you were told I had died. The Germans thought it would be useful to have the British think I was dead, so they orchestrated the whole scheme. I don't know who the men in that plane crash actually were. I think it was just a fortuitous accident."

"But the British don't think so, do they?" Ted's interruption was urgent. He didn't want Roger to be a fascist. "They know about you and you are really still spying for them? Right?"

"As I said before, Ted, it's a complicated world. Lines are not as clearly drawn as Will would like to think. But that is not what is important right now. Helmut believes that you should be shot."

"What?" Ted was shocked. Talking to his uncle had lulled him into assuming he was now safe. Suddenly the frightening image of the pigsty returned.

"I'm afraid so," Roger continued. "You see, Helmut thinks you have seen too much and that you might talk to the wrong people if you are sent home. But don't worry. I think I can persuade him to let you go. Then we can get you back into France."

"What about Dolores?"

"Dolores who?" asked Roger.

"Martinez. Dolores Martinez, my friend."

"So that is your companion's name. I was a little confused when I heard you had a sister. I'm afraid there is not much I can do there. She is Spanish. To get her released would be seen as interfering in local matters. I can't do that."

"Then I'm not going." The violence of Ted's denial surprised him. "If she's staying then I'm staying." Ted was terrified at what he was saying. If Dolores's fate was to be played out in the mud of the pigsty, then he was volunteering to share it with her. Ted shivered, but he was firm. "Dolores is my friend. She came to help me find Will and I will not desert her."

"Do you realize what you are saying?" Roger leaned forward and looked intently at Ted. "This is a war—a Spanish war. Despite whoever is involved from outside it remains a civil war. There is intense hatred on both sides. The officer in charge here has a sister who was a nun at a convent in Barcelona. He has heard that the convent was burned and all the nuns killed by the anarchists. When his men capture anarchists, he has them shot.

"This is a violent time. Once the officer examines your case and realizes that your friend is not your sister, I doubt if there is anything anyone will be able to do for her. If you choose to remain with her, you will be choosing to share her fate, and that will be a waste."

Ted noticed that his hands were shaking. It would be so easy to say okay and let himself be whisked to safety across the French border. After all, why sacrifice himself if he could do nothing to change fate? Then he remembered Dolores's eyes. He had been right, there was no way out.

"I love her," he said quietly, "if she stays, I stay."

Roger shook his head slowly and sat back.

"Stubborn like your father," he said. Then, abruptly he stood up and strode to the door. Opening it he shouted in Spanish for the soldier who had brought Ted. Roger gave him some brief instructions, then turned to his nephew, "It's your decision. I don't know what I can do. You will have to go back to the jail now."

Ted stood up and shakily walked to the door. As he passed his uncle Roger muttered one word, "Sorry."

Saturday, July 25, 1936
Evening

Ted was at the bottom of the stairs when he heard the rifle shots.

"Dolores!" he screamed sprinting past his startled guard, out the door and across the courtyard. He ignored the raised Spanish voices behind him. The courtyard was quieter than before with only small groups of soldiers lounging here and there in the sun. No one made a move to stop him. A truck, which Ted hadn't seen before, was parked beside the barn door. As he neared the milkshed, the guard outside made a grab for him. Ted lowered his head and drove it into the man's belly. The soldier grunted and fell sideways.

The door to the prison was heavy and locked, but Ted beat on it with his fists anyway. Rough hands grabbed his shoulders and swung his writhing body away from the door. Soldiers held Ted firmly while the guard picked himself up and unlocked the door. Ted was facing the hacienda now, breathing heavily. As he looked up, he saw a single figure standing at a first floor window watching.

Several soldiers gathered round. One made a remark in

Spanish which caused the others to laugh. Finally, the prison door opened and Ted was pushed unceremoniously into the gloomy interior. Half-blind from the bright sun, he looked around frantically.

"Dolores," he said, stumbling forward.

"Ted," a familiar voice replied. The pair embraced and slid down against the wall.

"I heard the shots," Ted began, "I thought…"

"Yes," said Dolores, "they came for some of the men. I thought you might have been with them." The pair lapsed into relieved silence. Eventually, Dolores asked, "What happened?"

"My uncle is here," Ted began, "and a German man."

"Your uncle, he is a fascist?"

"No, I don't think so. I don't know," Ted replied, shaking his head. "It's all so confusing. I don't know who to trust anymore."

"Can he help us?" Dolores was looking intently at Ted. Ted thought over what Roger had said.

"No, I doubt it," he said slowly. He was just about to outline his conversation with Roger, when the door opened. Four names were read out, but Dolores and Ted were not among them. Four figures stood reluctantly and slowly made their way out the door, which closed behind them with a horrible finality. There were five militiamen left. No one said a word. After what seemed like a lifetime, but

could only have been ten or fifteen minutes, the prisoners
heard a muffled volley of rifle fire. Dolores tensed. The volley was followed by four single shots. Ted realized he was
sweating despite the cool air. He heard Dolores sobbing
quietly and pulled her close to him.

They sat that way for a long time. At last the door opened
again. The names of five strangers echoed round the small
room. Then, "Dolores Martinez." Then, "Aydooard Reean."
Ted felt incredibly calm as the figures rose around him and
headed for the door. Dolores stopped sobbing. Arm in arm
the two friends followed the militiamen into the sunshine and
towards the pigsty.

There were three guards—two led the way and one
walked beside Ted and Dolores in the rear. The third soldier
seemed very clumsy; he kept jostling Ted, stepping in front
of them both. The pair stumbled along awkwardly and soon a
gap opened up between them and the five others. Ted wished
the guard would just leave them alone. It seemed unnecessarily cruel to make this final walk difficult.

The truck was still parked in front of the barn doors.
There was very little room between its dropped tailgate and
the barn wall and the group had to form a single file to
squeeze through. The others had already passed through by
the time Ted and Dolores arrived. As Dolores led the way, the
guard reached over Ted's shoulder and grabbed her roughly
by the arm. Urgently he whispered something in Spanish.

Dolores stopped and looked back.

"Rápido, rápido!" the man hissed. To Ted's surprise, Dolores hauled herself onto the truck's tailgate.

"Come on," she said, "quickly."

Confused, Ted pulled himself up and followed Dolores into the dark interior. The soldier slammed the tailgate closed and disappeared. Inside the truck was full of wooden boxes with white lettering stencilled on their sides. Ted could make out word *"munición."* Dolores moved as far forward as she could to a space near the front of the truck where they could both sit hidden from a casual glance in the back.

Scared to make any noise and not daring to hope too much, the pair sat in silence listening to the noises of the courtyard. Both shivered at the inevitable rifle volley which sounded very close. They held their breaths every time footsteps crunched on the gravel nearby, but no one paid the truck any attention. Ted's mind was screaming. Why had the soldier put them in the truck? Why had no one come looking for them when they didn't turn up at the pigsty? Was there a chance for them to escape or were they just postponing the inevitable? The uncertainty and the waiting were almost unbearable. Then Ted heard a familiar voice coming from the side of the truck near his head.

"Don't move. Keep quiet." It was Uncle Roger. "The truck will be leaving shortly for the front. The guard was bribed, but the truck driver doesn't know you're here. He won't check his load, but you will have to get out before he stops. The best place is about a mile from here when he has to slow down for a series of sharp corners. Drop out the back and go to the right so the driver won't see you. Hide until dark and then head east. The lines are fluid and confused, so you have a chance of getting through. Be careful not to be shot by the other side. Good luck."

Ted looked at Dolores. Hope. He squeezed her hand, she smiled back. Moments later the canvas flap was pulled down and secured and they were plunged into almost total darkness. Footsteps, the sound of a door slamming, then the truck's engine shuddered into life. The vehicle slowly began to move.

Once Ted was sure they were on the road, he made his way to the back of the truck. It was not easy crossing the bumpy interior and he had several new bruises by the time he was in a position to undo a corner of the canvas and peer out. He was relieved to see no one in sight. The air was thick with dust and the road flashed past below him with unnerving speed. He felt Dolores arrive at his side.

Ted guessed they were moving at about thirty miles an hour—too fast to jump. Roger had said the truck would slow down in a mile or so. At this speed, that would be in a couple of minutes. Ted moved to the right-hand corner of the truck and undid another section of the canvas cover. Looking to the side, he saw endless rows of olive trees. The sun was directly overhead, providing no clue as to where east was; however, Ted assumed the road ran approximately in that direction. If it was clear tonight Ted knew he could find the Pole Star and navigate roughly by that.

Ted's navigational musings were interrupted by the truck slowing down. The driver crunched down the gears and swung the vehicle into a tight, right-hand curve. They seemed to be climbing the flank of a low hill and the olive trees were dropping off below them. The landscape, at least what Ted could see through the dust, was becoming more rugged with jagged outcrops of gray limestone poking through the thin soil. This was not the way they had marched in after their capture. The driver must be taking a different road. Ted's sense of direction vanished. He would have to wait till nightfall. But first they needed to get out of the truck.

The driver crunched another gear and swung into the next corner. "Go right," Ted said, beckoning to Dolores as he swung his legs over the tailgate and stood on the fender. They had slowed down a lot, but the ground still seemed to be rushing past at a horrible pace. "Best not to think about it," Ted thought as he stepped off into thin air. He hit the ground running, but to little avail. After two rushed steps, Ted's body overtook his feet and he crashed down into the dust of the road. He rolled to a painful stop, sat up and looked for Dolores. She was lying on the road several yards ahead of him. She wasn't moving.

Scrambling to his feet, Ted hurried to her side. To his immense relief she was conscious and beginning to sit up. The dust was thinning and the truck was out of sight, its engine already a distant hum.

"Come on," Ted urged, offering Dolores his hand, "we have to get off the road."

Dolores stood up. The ground beside the road was rocky and sloped away sharply. Large rocks were scattered about, wherever they had ended their violent journey from the hillside above. The valley far below was filled with regular lines of trees.

"We must find a place to hide, wait until nightfall and then head east," said Ted, mimicking Roger's advice in what he hoped was a confident tone. Dolores nodded. Ted scanned the hillside looking for a likely hiding place. There were several rocky outcrops, some of which might have overhangs or shallow caves where they would be less conspicuous than out on the open slopes. His thoughts were distracted by the distant hum of a truck. It seemed to be getting louder. Puzzled, Ted cocked his head to one side. The sound was coming from down the hill.

"Something's coming," he yelled unnecessarily loudly. Grabbing Dolores by the arm, he jumped off the road and made for the nearest rock. Running untidily over the rough ground, Ted prayed neither of them would trip and sprain an ankle. The rock appeared far away, and the sound of the approaching vehicle was becoming very loud. Panting in the heat, Ted barely managed to thrust Dolores behind the rock and flatten himself against its sharp surface, before he saw the dark shape of an open car turn the last corner and climb towards them.

Roger and the tall blond German sat in the back, and the car was being driven by the third man Ted had glimpsed in the barn. The German looked straight ahead, but Roger scanned the landscape around him. Ted squeezed himself against the rock as the car passed uncomfortably close above him and was safely out of sight. Feeling dangerously exposed despite the rock's shelter, Ted rapidly plotted a course from boulder to boulder towards a larger rock outcrops some distance away.

"I think our best bet is over there," he said, indicating his route to Dolores. She nodded. The pair set off across the slope, pausing at each new rock to listen for traffic. The road remained silent.

Ted was a bit disappointed when they reached their new sanctuary. He had hoped for a small cave and there was none, but at least the outcrop had an overhang, which placed them in a shadow and made them hard to see from the valley below. More importantly, the shadow protected them from the cruel glare of the sun. Even so, the day was hot and they had no water. It would be a long, dry wait until dark.

Ted was surprised to hear Dolores laugh. Looking over he

saw his companion regarding him with a broad smile on her face. She looked like a happy ghost. Her skin, hair and clothes were covered with a layer of fine gray dust from which only her white teeth and dark eyes shone. She had a small cut on her forehead below which a tiny trickle of congealing blood carved a small line through the dust.

"Today is the day of the pilgrimage to the tomb of St. James," she said. "You look like a pilgrim who has crawled across Spain on his knees to pay homage."

"You look like a baker," Ted replied returning her smile, "a baker who fell in the flour barrel."

They both laughed, more at the relief of tension than the weak jokes. They were still in danger, and a long way from safety, but the immediate terrors of the pigsty had receded. By some unspoken mutual agreement, neither of them mentioned the horror they had witnessed that morning, although it was never out of their minds for long. Ted told Dolores what had happened with Roger. Dolores told Ted that the soldiers in red berets were Carlist *requetes*—Navarese supporters of the Carlist pretender to the throne—who sided with the army because they hoped it would restore the monarchy. The Carlists had plunged Spain into civil war in the previous century with their attempts to overthrow the legitimate king.

"I thought the rebels were unified," said Ted when she had finished. "They certainly seem well-organized."

"Nothing in my country is simple," Dolores answered.

"The fascists are just as mixed as we are. The army wants law and order; the Falange want pure fascism like Hitler and Mussolini; the Monarchists want the king back; the Carlists want the pretender on the throne; and the landowners and Church want a return to the old ways. Each group believes its idea is the right one for Spain and each is prepared to bathe the country in blood to achieve it. The rebels are no better organized than the anarchists. You can bribe or threaten a Spaniard, put him in uniform, teach him how to march and look pretty on a parade ground, but underneath it all he still has the heart of a farmer and the soul of a poet. That is not a combination that makes a good soldier."

After her explanation, they sat in silence for a while. Ted found himself daydreaming of cool mountain springs.

"I suppose we should try to get a couple hours of sleep," he said at length, "we can't go anywhere until dark and we will be traveling all night."

"Yes, you are right," Dolores replied, shifting to find a more comfortable position.

Sleep was a good idea, but a hard one to put into practice—the thirst, heat and discomfort made it almost impossible. However, Ted did manage to doze off several times, only to be awoken by vehicles on the road above. Nothing stopped. Ted noticed that Dolores was catnapping as well.

Saturday, July 25, 1936
Night

⟡———————⟡

Ted and Dolores awoke together as the last of the sun slipped behind the rugged hills. Ted was uncomfortable and very thirsty. His tongue was thick and furry and his stomach growled incessantly. From the setting sun's position, Ted figured that east was more-or-less straight across the low, flat ground in front of them. Finally, it was almost dark enough to travel. Though only a couple of stars were visible, finding water was a priority and Ted suspected that there might be a stream in the valley below.

Moving carefully from rock to rock, the two fugitives worked their way down the hillside. Occasionally one of them dislodged a rock which rattled and bounced away with an almost deafening noise. At last the slope eased and they were among the trees. They almost walked right past the stream. Ted had imagined a little babbling brook with cool, clear water in which they could wash off the grime of the day. What they found was a dry bed that barely formed a dip in the landscape. The pair would have walked right by, if Dolores's foot hadn't sunk into wet sand.

As her foot squelched down, Dolores fell against Ted, lucky not to twist her ankle. Looking down, the pair noticed an elongated darker patch of muddy sand in the longer depression of what had probably been a stream last winter.

"It is dry," said Dolores despondently.

Ted's vision of a babbling brook vanished. Then he brightened. "Maybe not," he said. Remembering the western novels he had read back home, Ted crouched down beside the stream bed and began to scoop out a hollow. In his stories, the hero's hollow always filled with crystal clear water and there was always plenty for him and his trusty horse to drink. After much digging, Ted's hollow was only a shallow muddy puddle. Still, it was water and Ted generously offered the first sip to Dolores. The water was gritty and had a strong earthy taste, but it did assuage their thirst. They also used some to wash the dust off their faces.

By the time they had finished, it was dark enough for Ted to make out the shape of the Big Dipper low in the northern sky. Lining up the two indicator stars, he traced his pointing finger over to the Pole Star.

"That's north," he said confidently. "So that must be east," he added, swinging his arm ninety degrees to the right to indicate a course through the trees. If he kept the Pole Star over his left shoulder, they shouldn't go too far off course. There was a good moon so they had enough light by which to travel, but not enough, Ted hoped, to be seen.

"We'd better get going," he said at last. "We don't know how far it is to the lines."

"Yes," agreed Dolores, "we have a busy night ahead of us."

For the first couple of hours they walked in silence through the olive groves. Ted's body ached all over and his hunger was almost unbearable but, after the events of the day, to be doing something—anything—felt good. It was spooky walking through the dark, twisted shapes of the old olive trees not knowing what was behind them. Ted could not shake his fear of stumbling into a fascist camp, but nothing happened and they made rapid progress.

Eventually, the ground became more rocky and began to rise. The trees thinned. Soon they were out on a bare hillside. Despite his earlier trepidation of the imagined dangers hidden behind them, Ted missed the trees. He felt exposed on the open slope even though it was probably too dark for anyone to see them, unless that person was also close enough to hear their increasingly labored breathing.

After climbing for about half an hour, the tired pair crested a ridge and sat down for a short rest. In front of them, bathed in moonlight, lay a steep-sided, rugged valley. Across from them was a ridge similar to the one they had just climbed. It looked as if they would have to cross a series of such ridges. Ted missed the olive trees and the flat ground even more.

As soon as they caught their breath, the two set off once

more, climbing and descending rocky ridges for what seemed like an eternity. Some places were so steep that they were forced to crawl on all fours. Once they found a dry gully which they could follow, but mostly they were in the open. Ted was surprised to find that going downhill was often harder than climbing uphill. Downhill was easier on the lungs, but after a while Ted's knees began to complain bitterly and he felt his leg muscles weakening. His thirst was also returning with a vengeance, and there was no sign of any damp sand. To make their work even harder, the moon set and they had to struggle over the rough ground in complete blackness.

Ted was stumbling, in little more than a daze, across the top of the fourth or fifth ridge, when he heard the cough. Instantly he froze. His tiredness vanished and he became unnaturally aware of his surroundings. Dolores, who had obviously heard the noise too, stood silent and immobile beside him. The sound seemed to come from Ted's left, but from how far away was impossible to tell. Ted crouched down and listened intently.

All Ted could hear was silence. He was beginning to stiffen and had almost convinced himself that he had imagined the noise when he heard another sound—metal against metal, as if someone had banged a tin cup against something heavier. Another cough sounded frighteningly close. But who? Was it a fascist unit or had they crossed the lines in the dark and were listening to a tired anarchist guard?

The fugitives had no way of knowing. Ted turned to look at Dolores. Her face was pale against the dark. Ted could barely saw her arm pointing past him.

Turning to look in the direction of Dolores's outstretched arm, Ted could make out the silhouette of the next ridge against a narrow strip of paler sky. Dawn was coming. The last thing they needed was to be caught in daylight, in the open, in the middle of the fascist lines. They would have to go on. With luck they could make it to the next ridge before it became too bright. If they didn't, they could find somewhere to hide in the valley below. If these were the fascist lines, then the next ridge should be held by the government. If they had crossed the fascist lines, then the next ridge would take them deeper into friendly territory.

Leaning over, Ted tapped Dolores on the shoulder and pointed down the slope. She nodded. Very slowly and very carefully, they began to inch their way down. It was painfully slow-going, but they could not risk making noise. Ted was convinced the guard could hear his footsteps as he dislodged tiny stones, but there was no response.

By the time they were halfway down, both felt comfortable enough to move faster. If the guard hadn't heard them a few feet away, he was unlikely to hear them a hundred yards down the slope. He was more likely to see them in the increasing light. Ted could just make out Dolores's shape in front of him. He did not see the dark shape detach itself from a rock ahead, grab Dolores and pull her to the ground. All he heard was the small avalanche of stones let loose by the scuffle and Dolores's muffled cry. Instinctively, Ted ran a step forward to help his friend. That was what saved him. The soldier who tried to grab him from behind was a fraction too late. His hands brushed roughly past Ted's shoulders, and merely knocked him off balance. Stumbling, Ted turned to face this new danger.

The soldier had recovered and was coming at Ted, but he was at a disadvantage. He was coming down the slope and had to crouch to catch what could only be a vague shape in front of him. Ted had a much clearer view of the soldier's silhouette against the lightening sky. Lunging upward, Ted swung his fist as hard as he could at the man's head. The solid connection sent a painful shudder up Ted's arm. The soldier slipped and fell pulling Ted on top of him. Frantically, the boy groped where he thought the soldier's head should be. His hands found hair. Grabbing tightly, Ted began to beat the man's head against the ground. The soldier was hitting him painfully in the side, but Ted kept on with almost manic concentration. Eventually, the blows to his side subsided and Ted felt the body beneath him go limp.

Not stopping to discover if the man was unconscious or dead, Ted scrambled off to help Dolores. There was no need. The soldier who had grabbed her was rolling on the hillside clutching his stomach and crying in pain.

The fight had only lasted seconds, but already there was the crackle of rifle fire from above. A loud explosion echoed from the slope to their right. Clutching Dolores's hand, Ted stumbled down the slope. None of the bullets came close to them and Ted assumed the guards were firing blindly into the dark. The explosions—caused by what Ted guessed were hand grenades—continued, but farther up the hill. All the attention seemed to be directed over the valley to the east at what must be the government lines.

The going was rough over no-man's-land, and the pair were in constant danger of breaking an ankle, but in a remarkably short time, they reached the bottom of the valley. It was narrow and rocky, like all the others. Their pace slowed as they began climbing. Although still in the shadow of the hillside, the daylight was becoming quite bright. Ted could not believe they had not been spotted. His back was beginning to itch where he expected a bullet to find him any minute. The slope ahead was impossibly long and difficult. All of a sudden, Ted heard a loud *zeeeee* as a bullet ricocheted uncomfortably close to his head. They had been seen.

Panting with exertion, they struggled on. Ted's lungs were on fire and every labored breath was agony. His muscles hurt and he felt sickeningly weak. He had to make a conscious effort to order each leg to make the next step. Dolores, close beside him, was suffering just as much. But they had to keep going. Ted hoped that there were friends at the top of the hill who didn't think they were part of a fascist attack.

The pair were now several hundred yards from the fascist positions but the number of bullets bouncing off the hillside around them was increasing. Dolores was right, Ted thought vaguely and thankfully, Spaniards are lousy shots. A huge foot kicked him hard on the left shoulder. Time slowed and Ted had an extraordinarily clear vision of the ground coming up to meet his face. Every tiny pebble was sharply outlined. He even had time to hope that a particularly large and sharp one wouldn't hit him in the face. Then he was on the ground. Ted's face missed the large stone, but he did get a mouthful of dust. He knew he had to get up, but he just didn't feel like it. A gentle blackness—like a thick woolen blanket—was drawing itself over him. At last he could rest. Thankfully, Ted closed his eyes.

Sunday, July 26, 1936
Sunrise

When he came to, Ted's first thought was how nice it was not to be forcing his tired legs on any more. If only that annoying bee would stop popping and buzzing around him, he would be quite happy just lying there and resting.

Ted was vaguely aware of a figure kneeling by his head. It was Dolores. That was nice. He was very fond of Dolores—he would enjoy lying on the hillside with her. Ted smiled; Dolores was beautiful even if she was covered in dirt. Dolores didn't look happy though. Ted frowned in concentration. She was trying to say something. What was it? Something about having to get up. Ted's shoulder hurt where he had been kicked, but not too badly, and he was sure that the pain would go away if only he could rest. Who had kicked him anyway? It didn't seem like the sort of thing Dolores would do. He couldn't remember anyone else being around.

Dolores was being very annoying. She kept insisting that he get up. Ted didn't want to. Now Dolores was trying to drag him up the hill. She was pulling on his right arm. That was no good, the way to pull someone was to grab them under the armpits and lift. Ted opened his mouth to tell her. Nothing happened. That was odd. He tried to lift his left arm, but nothing happened there either. The arm was limp and dragging in the dirt, and his shoulder was really beginning to ache. If only he could rest for a while, then he would be okay.

Why couldn't Dolores just leave him alone? Alone with the bees. But bees don't make popping sounds and the buzzing didn't sound right. The bees sounded more like—he couldn't remember. This was annoying. There was something important in the back of his mind. Something about the bees and his shoulder. Maybe he had been stung and not kicked? Yeah, that was probably it, he had been stung. Of course, he had been stung before—there had been that time he had disturbed a nest down by the lake and his mom had counted 17 stings when he finally made it home. But those stings hadn't felt like this. A particularly annoying bee shot past his head with a loud *zeeee*. Now that really didn't *sound* like a bee. It sounded like a...bullet. That was it, they were bullets not bees. He hadn't been stung or kicked, he had been shot.

Ted headed back to reality through the dull curtain of pain in his shoulder. This wasn't the sharp sort of pain he had always imagined when he read stories about someone being shot. Ted's pain was a dull, general ache which covered his whole shoulder. He wondered if he was bleeding. By twisting his head he could look down at his useless arm bouncing beside him. There didn't seem to be any blood. He looked back up at Dolores. She was struggling to haul his dead weight up the rough hillside. They were moving dreadfully slowly. This was no good, he could manage better than this—after all, he hadn't been shot in the leg.

"Help me stand up," Ted croaked as loudly as he could. Dolores immediately stopped pulling and began lifting. By putting his good arm around her shoulder, Ted was soon upright and they began staggering up the hill. Bullets were still zipping off the rocks around them, but the brow of the ridge was just up ahead. Ted really did hope there were some friendly people up there.

The first one he saw didn't seem friendly. The man appeared from behind a large rock and pointed a rifle straight at Ted. It was a relief to see the red and black anarchist scarf, but neither Dolores or Ted liked the sight of the rifle. It would be a terrible shame to be shot by your own side. Ted felt like shouting, "Don't shoot, I've already been shot by the other side."

More usefully, Dolores shouted, *"Nosotros somos POUM,"* followed by what Ted assumed was a rapid explanation of what had happened and a request for a *"médico."* The militiaman raised his rifle and fired a deafening shot over their heads at the fascist lines. Then he swung his gun over his shoulder, took Dolores's place under Ted's arm and hauled him over the brow of the ridge. He wasn't gentle, but he was fast and soon Dolores and Ted were lying in relative safety. Ted noticed that there was quite a lot of firing going on as the anarchists answered the shots from across the valley. He felt vaguely cheered that so many people were responding to the attack on him. Gradually, however, the firing on both sides died away.

It was almost full daylight now, although the sun had yet to appear over the brow of the next ridge. Dolores bent over to examine Ted's shoulder. Ted noticed that there was some blood, but surprisingly little. It formed an irregular patch around a tattered hole in his shirt just below his collar bone. That was a good thing Ted reasoned. First it meant that he probably wasn't going to bleed to death. And second as his western novels were always emphasizing, it was good for the bullet to come out the other side of you. Perhaps, Ted assumed, because it wasn't much fun having someone going in to look for it.

Ted took in his surroundings. Anarchist militia were scattered over the hillside; some in small groups eating breakfast, others engaged in animated conversation. Along the ridge top were a series of shallow pits from which prone soldiers with rifles peered across the valley at the enemy. Some way off, a rough parapet had been constructed from piles of stones. Several men crowded behind it. Most were peering intently over the valley. One man, wearing a large pair of black headphones, was seated beside a radio fiddling with the dials.

As Ted watched, a figure left the parapet and came toward him. The man was not tall, but he was broad and obviously strong. He was wearing a brown leather coat and cap, and a large pair of binoculars hung around his neck. His face, Ted could see as the man approached, was rugged and weather-beaten, but Ted was surprised by the softness and innocence of the large brown eyes. Ted recognized the face instantly from the banner he had seen on the street in Barcelona. This was the fabled Buenaventura Durruti, the savior of Barcelona, the man who had robbed banks, and the man who had killed the Archbishop of Zaragoza.

Durruti looked down at Ted.

"So this is our little foreign volunteer who has been shot by the fascists," he said in heavily accented English. "It is a pity you cannot come with us to Zaragoza, but I promise I will shoot a few fascists for you on the way."

"Oh, that's okay," Ted replied weakly. "Please don't shoot anyone on my account."

"But we will," Durruti smiled. "We are building a new Spain—a free Spain—and the foundations will be the blackened stones of churches and the bodies of every priest, landlord and fascist we can find. The old world of privilege and authority must be torn down and destroyed before a new world of equality and freedom can dawn. Perhaps only a hundred of us shall survive, but I will lead them into Zaragoza and proclaim the new day."

Durruti stood imposingly over Ted, a dark, powerful shape with the rising sun behind him.

"But all that will be left will be ruins," Ted replied. He was suddenly very tired. The world this man described didn't sound like it would be a great place in which to live.

"We are not afraid of ruins," Durruti's voice rose. Now he was talking to the men scattered over the hillside, although none of them could probably understand what he was saying. "As workers we have always lived in slums. But, as workers, we can also build. It was the workers who built the palaces and cities of the kings and we can do it again, but for ourselves this time. Yes, we will inherit ruins, but we carry the world of the future in our hearts and in our hands."

Durruti stopped his speech and looked back at Ted.

"So maybe you will come and visit us when you are better," he said before turning and striding back to the parapet.

Ted nodded vaguely at Durruti's back. All he really wanted to do was sleep. The pain in his shoulder was becoming quite nasty. Its dull ache seemed to be radiating out from the wound in waves over his entire body. Ted's eyes were very heavy. The last thing he noticed was a man carrying a small, black doctor's bag hurrying across the hillside towards him. How strange, he thought just before he lost the battle with his eyelids, I didn't think anyone made house calls in a war.

Sunday, July 26, 1936
Day

⁊⁊————————⁊⁊

The journey down from the hills to the hospital in
Lérida was a nightmare. Fortunately, Ted was
unconscious for most of it, but dream-like images floated in
and out of his befuddled brain. The first one was the
strangest. In it Ted was held in place on a donkey by a large
anarchist as they made their way up and down rough paths.
Dolores was walking on the path ahead of him. At one point
they passed an open-air school. A few militia sat on the
ground in front of a large blackboard. Several letters of the
alphabet were written above a rough sketch of a trench. The
teacher, a woman in militia clothes, pointed at the letters
with a long stick as the class repeated them in raggedly.
Strange, thought Ted, it's the summer holidays, then he
lapsed back into unconsciousness.

The next thing Ted remembered was a church. He was on
a table with several figures gathered around and a man in a
grubby white coat poking at his shoulder. The shoulder still
hurt, but in a general way and Ted couldn't feel what the man
was doing. He heard several comments in Spanish and looked

around for Dolores to translate. She was nowhere to be seen and Ted felt unutterably sad.

When Ted awoke next, someone was screaming. This wasn't surprising since he was in an ambulance which appeared to be driven by the ghost of the mad German. Several wounded men were in the vehicle and all were being thrown around as the truck smashed unavoidably into the numerous potholes on the road. The man screaming was obviously in extreme pain. Ted wondered, with a kind of distant companionable concern, where he had been shot. His own wound still hurt but he was getting almost used to that. His main problem was that the jolting of the ambulance kept shaking his useless left arm off the cot, leaving it dangling in mid-air. Every time this happened, Dolores would reach over and gently place it back at his side. Ted was glad she was back. He smiled at her. Dolores smiled back, and Ted drifted off again.

Monday, July 27, 1936
Morning

❧————————————❧

Ted awoke in a bed. A real bed. The first one he had seen since Barcelona. Not that that was so long ago; although it seemed like a lifetime. The bed was comfortable. The sheets were cool and the ward was large, light and airy. Ted's shoulder was bandaged and his floppy arm finally brought under control by a sling which held it firmly across his chest.

Dolores was sitting in a chair beside the bed. She was clean and dressed in a new pair of blue overalls. The sun shone through the nearby window and glinted off her hair.

"Good morning."

"Good morning," Ted responded weakly. "Where am I?"

"In the hospital in Lérida," she answered. "We came down yesterday. You slept most of the way and all last night. How are you feeling?"

"Not bad," Ted replied, "but a bit unlucky, being shot so close to home."

"The doctors say you are very lucky. The bullet seems to have hit nothing major. Two inches down and it would have hit your heart."

"But what about my arm," Ted interrupted, "I can't move it."

"That will return. The bullet passed very close to a nerve and the shock numbed it. In a few days the feeling will come back. Already this morning I saw your fingers twitch."

Ted looked down at his fingers sticking out of the end of the sling. Experimentally he tried to move them. His thumb refused to respond, but the four fingers moved slightly.

"Couldn't catch a baseball though," he joked. Then more seriously, "Thank you for saving me."

Dolores blushed. "You saved me on the road when the fascist officer wanted to shoot me." The pair gazed at each other in silence for a moment.

"That was quite an adventure," Ted said at length. "What day is it?"

"Monday," Dolores answered.

"This is my fifth day in Spain," Ted mused wonderingly. It seemed like much longer. "And we still haven't found Will."

"I have," said Dolores happily.

"You have? How? Where is he?"

"I telephoned my father last night when we arrived here," Dolores continued. "He had heard that your father was in Barbastro, about seventy kilometers to the northeast. He said that he would get a message to your father that you were here. Perhaps he is already on his way."

"Thank you." Ted closed his eyes and sighed. He had said thank you, but, oddly enough, he wasn't sure he meant it. Will's arrival would mean that he would never see Dolores again. Why had she phoned her father? Couldn't they just have gone on having adventures with no responsibility except to themselves?

Ted felt suddenly that he had very little in common with his father. When he had seen the soldier grab Dolores on the hillside, he had reacted instinctively. When the soldier had grabbed at him, Ted had fought back without thinking, and he had kept on fighting until he had won. Ted might even have killed the man. Ted could never call himself a pacifist again. Perhaps Roger was right. Perhaps violence was sometimes justified if a thing was worth fighting for. Dolores and all the soldiers he had met in the last five days certainly thought so. Every one of them was prepared to die for their beliefs. In the past few days, Ted had almost been killed several times, yet he couldn't remember feeling more alive—or happier.

Waves of guilt swept over Ted as he thought of his mother lying unconscious in her hospital bed in Perpignan. He had come to Spain for her—for his whole family. Keeping his family together had been his only goal. Why did he have to lose something so valuable to achieve it? It seemed horribly unfair. Why was life so complicated?

Ted opened his eyes to find Dolores watching him. He held out his hand. Dolores took it.

"Ted," she began slowly, "soon, I think, you will be going back home. I have never felt more fright, nor more excitement, than in the days we have just spent. I hope one day you will come back when there is peace here and I will show you the beauty of my country without the guns and the blood."

"I would like that and maybe you could come to Canada, and I will show you the orchards around my home."

"Yes," she replied, "I would very much like that too," then more seriously, "but for now I must stay. There is much work to be done if we are to keep our freedom. But there are many brave people to help us and I am sure we will win."

Ted shuddered as he remembered what Roger had told him. He was saved from a reply by a commotion in the corridor. A voice he recognized was saying, "My son is here somewhere, and I intend to find him." A tall, familiar figure appeared in the doorway surrounded by an agitated group of nurses. Ignoring them, Will made his way over to Ted's bedside. Dolores relaxed Ted's hand and slipped to the foot of the bed. Ted's eyes followed her, but the shape of his father moving in for a hug, obscured his view.

"Thank God you're all right," said Will pulling back. "I received a message last night from Rafael saying you were here. I hitched a ride this morning on an ammunition truck.

The message said that Catherine was sick and you were wounded. What happened?"

"I'm okay," Ted began. "I was shot in the shoulder, but the bullet missed anything vital. Dolores dragged me to safety." Ted indicated the figure at the foot of his bed.

Turning, Will acknowledged her presence.

"I'm sorry," he said, "it was rude of me to barge past you, but I was so shocked to see Ted here. You must be Dolores Martinez." Will held out his hand. "I am sorry I missed you when I saw your father in Barcelona. Thank you for saving Ted."

Dolores took Will's hand.

"I was merely repeating what he did for me."

Will held her eyes for a moment then turned back to Ted.

"What about your mother? The message said something about a head injury."

Slowly, Ted told the whole story of what had happened in Perpignan after Will had left. It seemed like ancient history. Will listened intently with a frown on his face. Ted said nothing about what had happened after he had met Rafael Martinez. There would be plenty of time for that later.

"Well," said Will, "we will have to get back to Perpignan as quickly as possible. The truck I came on is heading for Barcelona. The driver is waiting. Can you travel?"

"I think so," replied Ted looking at Dolores. She nodded. "I certainly seem to be well bandaged up, and I feel well enough."

"Good," said Will, "then let's get you dressed. I don't know how long that driver will wait. Will you come with us Miss Martinez?"

Both Will and Ted looked down the bed at Dolores. Slowly she shook her head.

"I do not think so," she replied. "I think I shall return to Leciñena, if the fascists have not taken it, and join the militia. I think I can be of most help there."

Ted was struck dumb. This was to sudden. He knew Will's arrival would mean saying good-bye to Dolores, but he had assumed she would return with them at least as far as Barcelona. Now she was going off to join the militia and maybe get killed.

"No," he said weakly, fighting back tears.

"I must Ted," said Dolores, gently moving round the bed to his side. "And you must go back to Canada with Will and your mother. I will never forget you, and one day you will come back and I will take you to a bullfight. It is a promise."

Dolores leaned forward and kissed Ted on the lips. Then she stood up. Ted could hardly see her through the tears welling in his eyes.

"Perhaps then there will be some good anarchist matadors," he choked out.

Dolores smiled, "Yes maybe there will. Good-bye, Ted."

"Good-bye, Dolores," and then so quietly he could never

be sure she heard him, he whispered "I love you."

Then she was gone and his whole world was empty.

In a daze, Ted got dressed as well as he could. Will helped, but had the sense to remain silent. There was nothing to say. Leaning on his father's arm, Ted made his way along the hospital corridors, down stairs, and into the truck which would take him away from the one person he never wanted to leave behind.

Monday, July 27, 1936
Afternoon

The truck ride to Barcelona was uneventful, if uncomfortable. Ted sat sandwiched between the silent Spanish driver and Will. His shoulder still hurt and he kept wanting to fall asleep; however, he managed to tell Will about his adventures behind the lines. His father listened intently without comment when Ted told him about his fight with the soldier. Then it was Will's turn.

"I did a lot of traveling, to the front, such as it is, and in the anarchist villages. They are truly extraordinary. There are no owners, all wealth is collectivized and shared out to whomever needs it. Something unusual is happening here, it is an ideal put into practice. I never believed anarchy could work, but here it is.

"I couldn't have understood the poverty here if I had not seen it. Yet the people appear happy and willingly share what little they have. Perhaps it is only because they have so little that collectivization is working. But it is still something worth protecting."

Will paused and gazed reflectively out at the barren

landscape.

"I must have just missed you in Leciñena. I was there only a few hours after the bombing raid. The fascists reached the edge of town. It turned out to be just a local affair, not even affecting the anarchist militia on either side. In fact, the next day, the POUM militias recovered most of the lost territory."

Ted wondered what had happened to the squad of soldiers that had captured Dolores and him. He wondered if someone had eventually found the dead soldier in the barn. That was something else to add to the growing list of things he would never know.

"For a while though," Will continued, "it looked like Leciñena might fall. I was in a house with half a dozen militia when it was attacked. Bullets were flying in through the windows, so I took cover behind an overturned table.

"There was a window beside me and a militiaman was firing his rifle over the sill. This man had accompanied me to the front that day and I had grown fond of him. He was poor and illiterate, but had a tremendous sense of wonder at the world around him. He wanted desperately to learn and was absolutely delighted when I took the time to teach him a few words of English. He went around for the rest of the day using them whenever he could, whether the words were appropriate or not. He told me through an interpreter that he wanted to attend one of the anarchist schools being set up at the front for the militia.

"Anyway, he was hit in the head while I was hiding behind the table. He fell backwards right beside me. I think he was dead before he hit the ground." Will took a deep breath and continued. "The sight of that dead soldier did something to me. He was so hopeful and innocent and here he was, lying beside me dead. I snapped. Without thinking, I picked up his rifle and stood at the window firing out. I couldn't see much, and I doubt very much if I hit anything. Still, I can never know. Perhaps we have both killed a man.

"Afterwards, I felt the most overwhelming guilt but, at the time, it seemed like I had had no choice. It was the obvious thing to do. Spain is so different right now. The normal rules don't seem to apply. Everyone does what the moment demands. And that is what I did. I am not proud of it, but at least now I realize that violence is a part of me. A part which must always be held in check, but which nonetheless must be acknowledged."

Will fell silent. Ted sat gazing at the familiar landscape rushing past. His father's story was incredible—he had actually fired a rifle in anger at another human being. An action that was against everything in which Will had ever believed. But his father was right. Spain was different than Canada, and it had the power to change people in fundamental ways. Both he and his father had changed, and they were going to have to learn to live with those changes. Both Will and Ted

were being forced to analyze their belief in pacifism. This
self-reflection was an easier job for Ted, who had just
accepted his father's position without fully understanding it.
It would be tougher for Will, who had lived with his carefully thought-out beliefs for years. But Ted had changed in
another way as well.

In only a few days, Ted felt as if he had aged ten years.
Not only physically, that would pass as his body recovered,
but emotionally and intellectually. Ted had met, fallen in
love with—and lost—an extraordinary girl who was on her
way to fight, and possibly be killed, in a war. Ted was cer-
tain that, whoever he met in the future, a part of him would
always belong to Dolores. How could any of the girls he
knew back home ever compare to her? They all seemed so
bland and uninteresting.

Dolores was different. She cared about important things,
the world about her and where it was going, and she was
prepared to do something to change that world for the better. Dolores was so beautiful. Ted could see her face with
those incredible eyes, hovering in the dust-laden air outside
the windshield of the truck. Clenching his fist hard in his
lap, Ted squeezed his eyes closed against the tears which he
couldn't prevent falling. He hoped and prayed his uncle
Roger was wrong and that the Spanish workers would win.
Then he could return and find Dolores again.

"She meant a lot to you didn't she?" Will's voice intruded into his thoughts.

"Yes," said Ted, turning helplessly to his father and wiping his cheeks. "She was...wonderful." What else could he say?

Will lifted his hand and moved it toward Ted's head. At the last minute, he dropped it onto Ted's good shoulder and gave a companionable squeeze.

"Don't worry," he said kindly but uselessly, "I'm sure she will be all right."

Ted smiled halfheartedly and returned his gaze out the window. How he wished he could be sure.

Tuesday, July 28, 1936

They were held up for a full day in Barcelona by Ted's lack of a passport. Without one, it would be impossible to get on the train. They would be stopped at the border and there would be all kinds of embarrassing questions. They might be delayed for days.

The alternative was to go to Madrid, report the passport missing and get a new one issued by the Canadian consul. But that too would take days, and Ted and Will were in a hurry.

Once more, Rafael Martinez came to the rescue. He had been upset about, but resigned to, the news that Dolores had joined the militia.

"I have been half expecting it for ages," Rafael said when Ted told him. "I dreaded it, but I learned from Dolores's mother that I could not control the women in my family and that they will do whatever they feel they must," he shrugged. "All I can do is give my blessing and pray she will come back unharmed."

He had listened intently as Ted related their adventures, and nodded when Will had explained their travel dilemma.

"I agree," he said. "Documents are a necessary evil and should not stand in the way of what we need to do. There are many trucks these days traveling to France with the products of our industry. They take heavy machinery and hope to bring back arms and ammunition. Mostly they return empty, but some precious loads have arrived. I will see if something can be done."

Then, turning to Ted, he added, "I must thank you for saving my daughter from the fascist officer. I am glad she was with you in that adventure. The least I can do is help to reunite your family."

For two nights, Will and Ted slept in the POUM dormitories at the bottom of Ramblas. The forced inactivity was hard; both were desperate to get back to the hospital in Perpignan and for Ted there was the added pain of revisiting the places he had been with Dolores. Ted even took Will for a bowl of snails at the Café Moka.

Ted was regaining his strength. His shoulder was improving and the feeling was rapidly returning to his left arm. By Tuesday evening he had regained much of its use, although his movement was limited by the pain. That evening as the sun was setting—painting the strollers on Ramblas a rich orange—Rafael Martinez arrived with the news that he had arranged passage for both on a truck heading into France. Ted would have to hide in the cargo, but the truck was leaving on Wednesday morning. The driver had agreed to drop the pair off in Perpignan on his way north.

Wednesday, July 29, 1936

Ted traveled in the truck's cab until close to the French border. Then Ted moved to a large wooden box containing heavy machine casings. He was cramped and uncomfortable, and the crate smelled strongly of oil and diesel fuel. The stop at the border was tense, but no one even looked in the back of the truck. Ted supposed the guards were more concerned about smuggling things into Spain rather than out of it.

As soon as they passed into France, Ted rejoined Will and the driver up front. Will had been very tense at the border, but, for Ted, it had been nothing after what he had been through. He knew that, even if he got caught, no one was going to shoot him.

The first view of the hospital in Perpignon as the truck drew up in front of it brought all his doubts rushing back to Ted. What had happened while he had been gone? Had Bernard kept his promise to look after his mother? What would they find; his mother sitting up and smiling at her family or, Ted shuddered, an empty bed?

Thanking the driver as rapidly as possible, Will and Ted hurried through the hospital doors. Without stopping to announce their presence, Ted led the way along the clean corridors to the ward where he had left his mother. His heart was pounding. They turned through the swinging doors to the ward. Ted stopped so abruptly that Will crashed into his back, almost knocking him over. His mother had been in the third bed along the wall on the left-hand side. That bed was empty. The sheets were neatly pulled up with the corner folded back ready to receive the next patient.

With mounting panic, Ted surveyed the rest of the ward. There was no sign of his mother. A nurse headed towards them. Ted stepped forward to meet her.

"Where is she?" he asked urgently, forgetting he was in France. The nurse looked puzzled.

"*Ma mère*," Ted tried again, pointing at the empty bed. The nurse shrugged and said something he didn't understand. Ted was close to panic.

"Where is she?" he shouted. Another nurse hurried down the ward to help her colleague. Ted felt Will's hand on his shoulder, but he shook it off. He moved forward: The nurse backed away. All the frustrations and terrors of the last week seemed to well up inside him. He had lost Dolores; there was no way he was going to lose his mother too. The nurse was beginning to look scared. Her companion hesitated. Again Ted felt Will's hands, more firmly this time, on his shoulders. His wound hurt. Behind him a rising babble of voices came from the door. Ted was helpless, almost out of control. He wanted to hit someone—anyone.

"You are back!" A familiar voice made Ted turn.

Bernard was striding toward him. As he got within range, Ted grabbed at the collar of his white coat.

"What happened to my mother?" he shouted. Bernard looked startled. Then he quickly regained his composure.

"She is all right," he said firmly and loudly. "She awakened on Sunday with nothing more than a sore head."

Ted's anger drained instantly and his body relaxed. His hand dropped away from Bernard's lapel. Will let go of his shoulders and stepped forward.

"I am Ted's father," he said extending a hand to Bernard. "Ted told me about you. We are very grateful for your help. Thank you. But where is my wife?"

Bernard took Will's hand in a firm grip. "Your wife was fine when she awoke, but she was a problem for us. She was not sick, and she had no identification, no papers, and no money to pay her bill. We did not know what to do. Fortunately, her brother arrived on Monday. He paid for her stay here and took her to a guest house in town. He left us a letter for you."

While he had been talking, Bernard had extracted a white envelope from his coat pocket. It was addressed to Will Ryan. Will took it and moved over to sit on the edge of the empty bed. Ted joined him. Bernard said something in French to the small crowd of nurses who had gathered at the commotion, and they dispersed. He stood waiting patiently while Will and Ted read Roger's note.

Dear Will, and I hope, Ted,

After I learned about Catherine, I made a detour to see if I could be of help. I had no idea of when you might be able to return and things are so complicated now. I was relieved to find her in excellent health although worried about you both. Bernard and his colleagues did a splendid job of looking after her, but it was obvious she could not stay in the hospital forever. I took the liberty of settling Catherine's bill and establishing her in the Pension Diderot at 15 Rue Saint Michel. Her bill there is paid for a week and I gave Catherine enough cash to attend to her basic needs for at least that long.

Unfortunately, I must move on. Pressing business. I am sure you understand. I am sorry, Will, that I did not get to meet you on this trip. I would have enjoyed our discussions and, perhaps, you might have found that we are not as diametrically opposed politically as you might think. The difference, I believe, is only your idealism against my pragmatism.

I hope you both managed to arrive here safely to read this. My recommendation is that you do not return to Spain in the foreseeable future. Paris in the summer is a nice place to wait while the Canadian consul replaces

Ted's missing passport. I would also be extremely grateful if you would not mention my presence, or even my existence, to anyone in authority. I am sure you understand the need for this secrecy.

Good luck. Have a safe journey home.

Roger

Will read the letter twice and turned the page over to see if there was anything on the back. Then he folded it neatly and replaced it in its envelope.

"Well," he said, turning to Ted, "shall we go and see your mother?"

"Yes," his son replied. "I think it's time to go home."

EPILOGUE
Sunday, September 5, 1999

⚬———⚬

I t was exactly five in the afternoon at the Plaza de Toros Monumental in the northern suburbs of Barcelona. Illuminated by the late sun, the matador and bull stood, immobile, as if carved from rock, in the center of the circle of sand. The matador, in his brightly-colored suit of lights, was leaning slightly forward. His cape was draped before him and his eyes were fixed on those of the bull. The bull stood several feet away, head lowered, and breathing heavily—his entire attention taken up with the twitching corner of the matador's cape.

Time was frozen. Ted held his breath. Everything he had done in the 77 years of his life—his adventures in Spain, his experiences in the Second World War fighting with the Canadian army to liberate Holland from the fascists, his struggle to establish a life and raise a family in a changing world—had all led to this one crystal moment. Ted was realizing his dream. He was at a bullfight.

Encouraged by an almost imperceptible flick of the cape, the bull charged. The matador swung the cape and, for a moment, a 500 kilogram fighting bull and a 75 kilogram fragile man were united inextricably within a single swirl of red cape.

Ted gasped at the beauty and artistry of the movement. Around him the crowd applauded. The woman in the seat to his right smiled. She reached over and squeezed his arm.

"It is good?" she asked. Ted nodded.

"You see," the woman continued, "even after all these years I still keep my promises."

Ted pulled his gaze away from the bullfight and looked at the woman. The face was old, but the dark brown eyes were the same ones he had fallen into that night in the barn so many years before. Ted returned her smile.

"Thank you," was all he could think of saying.

Ted could hardly believe he was sitting here watching a bullfight with Dolores by his side. Just as he had not believed, when he answered a knock on the door one day in 1946, that it was Dolores and her father standing on the step of his house in the Okanagan. But it had been. Through all her experiences of war, refugees, and occupation, Dolores had never let go of the vision Ted had given her of the peaceful lines of fruit trees along the shores of Okanagan Lake. After Hitler was finally defeated, she had come looking for him.

Now Spain was free, and Dolores had persuaded Ted to come back to her home so she could fulfill her promise.

Much had changed. All the people from that long ago time were gone—Will, Rafael, Catherine, the mysterious Roger, most of the enthusiastic shouting anarchists and the young fascist soldiers they had fought. All had been swallowed by time just as surely as the Carlist soldier in the barn.

A roar from the crowd brought Ted back to the present. In the ring the bull lay dead and the matador was waving his hat in acknowledgment of the applause. It was the last fight of the day and people were beginning to leave. To Ted's left a boy of fourteen sat gazing sadly at the scene before him. It was Ted's grandson, Will.

"What did you think?" Ted asked.

"It was spectacular," replied Will, "but it wasn't fair. The bull never really had a chance."

"True," Ted answered, "but it's not a hockey game with a different winner each time. It's much more complicated than that." He looked at Dolores and smiled.

"Anyway," he continued, "your grandmother and I know this little café in town. Let's go there for a plate of snails and we will tell you a story that happened a long time ago.

AUTHOR'S NOTE

Ted's and Dolores's adventures are based as closely as possible on fact. Some liberties have been taken with geography and time, but they are minor. What happened to the main characters in this story could have happened in Spain in 1936.

The Spanish Revolution and civil war were extraordinary events. They tore the country apart and polarized world opinion. But, Roger was right. The war in Spain did *not* lead to a general European war. Hitler sent large amounts of arms to help the rebels. He also sent his Luftwaffe as the Condor Legion. Many of the air crews who later bombed London and Rotterdam received their training in Spain. Mussolini also sent armaments and 50,000 fascist 'volunteers' who, much to his embarrassment, were routed by the smaller government forces at the battle of Guadalajara in 1937. Russia sent armaments and communist 'advisors' who ensured that the Spanish experiment in anarchy was doomed.

Britain, France, America, and Canada did nothing, even when their own vessels were torpedoed by Italian submarines in the Mediterranean. Canada's Prime Minister King continued to admire Hitler, characterizing him in his diary as "one who truly loves his fellow man."

Many workers from around the world felt that the

Spanish government's cause was worth defending and flocked to fight in the International Brigades. In early 1937, George Orwell served with a POUM militia in the hills outside Zaragoza and witnessed the communists suppressing the POUM in street fighting in Barcelona in May, 1937. He was based in the POUM headquarters on Ramblas while a squad of opposing Civil Guards held the Café Moka next door. He wrote about his experiences brilliantly in *Homage to Catalonia*.

Despite the Canadian government making it illegal for Canadians to go and fight in Spain, many ignored the law and went. These volunteers included Norman Bethune, who took a mobile blood transfusion unit to the front. In all, some 1600 Canadians fought in Spain. Half of them never returned.

The Spanish Civil War came to an end on April 1, 1939, with the victory of the rebels under General Francisco Franco. It would be five months before the rest of Europe decided something had to be done to put a stop to fascism. Franco's regime outlasted Hitler's and Mussolini's by thirty years, but finally ended in 1975. Spain is now a democracy and all those foreigners who fought for the government in the International Brigades have been awarded honorary Spanish citizenship.

The main characters in this story are fictitious but what happened to them was all too real. People like Dolores and her father would have fled to France at the end of the Spanish

War. Living in refugee camps, they would have soon become involved in the German occupation and, perhaps, they might have been active in the resistance. In 1945, they could have applied to come to Canada as refugees and that is how Dolores might have ended up on Ted's doorstep.

Ted would have returned to Canada in 1936 where his wound would have healed quickly. Ironically, both Ted Ryan and Henry Thomas would have been old enough to go to war to fight Hitler. Maybe they met fighting a common enemy in Italy, France or Holland. Maybe in that shared experience, Henry saw the error of his ways.

Buenaventura Durruti is real and many of the words he spoke to Ted on the hillside are paraphrases of comments he actually made to journalists. He really did kill the Archbishop of Zaragoza in 1923, but he never led the last hundred of his militia into the same town. Zaragoza remained throughout the war in rebel hands, often within tantalizing sight of the government lines, its lights shining at night, as Orwell put it, "like the portholes of a great long liner."

In November, 1936, Durruti took his militia to defend Madrid where he hoped their valour would bring him more honor. Their first attack failed when the militiamen refused to face the heavy machine-gun fire of their Moorish opponents. Incensed, Durruti promised an attack for the following day. Unfortunately, the Moors attacked first and the anarchists broke and fled. Only the intervention of the first International

Brigades of foreign volunteers saved the day. On November 20, while the battle for Madrid still raged, Durruti was shot and killed. Some say he died from a stray bullet. Others say he was shot in the back by his own men. History, you see, like life, is rarely simple.

JOHN WILSON is the author of *Across Frozen Seas* (Beach Holme, 1997), *Weet's Quest* (Napoleon Publishing, 1997), and *Weet* (Napoleon Publishing, 1995). *Across Frozen Seas* was shortlisted for the Sheila Egoff Book Prize and the Geoffrey Bilson Award for Historical Fiction. It was also an "Our Choice" selection of the Canadian Children's Book Centre. *North with Franklin: The Lost Journals of James Fitzjames*, a novel for adults, was published in 1999 by Fitzhenry & Whiteside. John lives in British Columbia with his family.